Disconnection

Claude Ollier

Disconnection

Translated by Dominic Di Bernardi

Dalkey Archive Press

Originally published by Flammarion, 1988

Library of Congress Cataloging in Publication Data
Ollier, Claude.
  [Déconnection. English]
  Disconnection / Claude Ollier; translated by Dominic Di Bernardi.
  Translation of: Déconnection.
  1. World War, 1939-1945—Fiction. I. Title.
PQ2675.L398D4413 1989   843'.914—dc20   89-35215
ISBN: 0-916583-47-3

First American Edition

Partially funded by grants from The National Endowment for the Arts and The
Illinois Arts Council.

Dalkey Archive Press
1817 North 79th Avenue
Elmwood Park, IL 60635 USA

*Printed on permanent/durable acid-free paper and bound in the United States
of America.*

Disconnection

He knows that memory will betray him. Later on. Will deceive, will delude him.

Will distort the scenes, shuffle their order.

Knows it already. Has learned this, already.

Knows that what in this place he sees, hears, will be poorly safeguarded, poorly protected, poorly restored. Will be mixed up, later on.

Dashed, riddled. Or erased.

But Martin isn't any less observant. All eyes: facades, banderoles, posters; towers, walls, old roofs.

But listens that much more keenly, all ears, to fix the locations, as far as possible, save these sounds, fanfares, trolley bells, clicking footsteps.

Hears the voice in the distance, from the loudspeaker, already hears the noise. Seemingly hears it, hasn't reached the Ring yet, from this point hears only voices calling, the din of motors, shouts.

Passes the Ring a little farther on and the deep ditch, Marientor, the door in the ramparts, ears pricked up, picks up the pace, stepping quickly.

The real voice now, funneled inside the old street, a summer mist on the cobblestones of Lorenzstrasse, slick and glistening, a dampness, a recent shower.

At the bend in the street catches sight of the church, massive, with golden spires, Lorenzkirche, its nave damaged.

Goes around the edifice and returns to the main street, Königsstrasse, the people on the sidewalk, in small groups, seem less
hurried than he, on their way down to the river.

Others pass on bicycles, in boots, feathered hats, rare cars, five
o'clock, today the factories closed earlier, the stores, the offices.

Doesn't believe his eyes, Martin simply finds himself here, in
this city, not quite one whole week, walking on these cobblestones, he too going down toward the river, can spot the bridge,
soon crosses the flower-decked bridge.

The voice is everywhere now, fills the square, the old city
center, indeed that's the voice, that's the one. Emphatically
bursts forth, rings out, echoes.

When he comes into the square, Goebbels has already begun to
speak. He's there on the platform, with the dignitaries, green
overcoat, has kept on his cap, too big for him, face furrowed,
obstructed by the microphones, shouts very loudly.

Doesn't believe his ears, what's happening to him, this tribune
seen so often before the war on screens, newsreels of childhood,
adolescence, here in motion, very close, brandishing a fist,
renowned actor, self-assured, haranguing at the top of his lungs.

Behind him the pennants, around him, standards, banners,
ritual trappings, the weapons of the party, the province, mobilized coats of arms, the escutcheons of cities and guilds, medieval
paraphernalia to the rescue.

Tried and tested stagecraft, fetishistic, harking back to bygone
myths, the noble deeds of knighthood, rustic orders, the small
dry man is there, contorted, assumes this glamour, bestows it
upon himself, glacial, reads from his paper.

Martin emboldened slips in, to his surprise the square is not
jammed, gaps between the groups, reaches within a few yards of
the tribune, closely observes, closely notes, giving the impression he was sent for that express purpose, to be a witness, to
observe closely.

Doesn't understand everything, nowhere near that. Clearly
pronounces, the orator, articulates precisely, speaks too quickly,

but the themes are simple, the clichés tired, easy to guess, to interpolate.

The theme concerns an act of treason, a treacherous king, the Latin ally has laid down its weapons, has turned its weapons upon us, the shame upon its name, we are true to our faith and our morale remains high, of a different caliber.

Functional, measured mimicking: the right forearm, fist clenched, back-and-forth horizontally, very quickly, level with the heart, folded back, straightened out, touches the heart rhythmically.

Then the left arm rises, half bent, the fist still clenched, hammers frenetically, vertically, each syllable enunciated, strongly emphasized, a sober programmed crescendo.

Fists on hips at last, stands on tiptoe, and the puny man, a trifle rachitic, calls to witness, ears sticking out, those two deep furrows carving his cheeks, hooked nose, a studied fanatic.

Proclaims in front of himself, in every direction, far in front, questions total war, do you want it, the shortest war, the time is now, long live victory! hail victory! victory, hail!

He extends his arm, Martin watches the arms extend, slanting, hands raised, automatic allegiance, unrestrained approval, how to know, a soldier on leave in front of him doesn't raise his arm, the woman at his side, arm extended, urges him, he makes a motion with his hand, disenchanted, drops it.

A glance around, the few soldiers present don't raise their arms, somewhat lost in the crowd, doesn't the minister see them, that they're not saluting? For civilians this diatribe, for civilians to stand fast, those in the bombed factories, the cities under attack already.

Noise, the crowd in chorus, again taking up the hymn, sings solemn, contemplative, Haydn's theme, familiar andante, great posthumous success.

Fills the square, baroque facades, brasseries, Marienkirche under sandbags, and the fountain, Schöner Brunnen, invisible, buried in sand too.

The arms fall, and the mark of fervor, final salute, Goebbels is gone already, has stolen off, the gathering drifts apart, slow U-turns, no enthusiasm, some believe it of course, hard as iron, others are no doubt resigned, see in this the war coming to a perhaps quick end.

Martin, disconcerted, follows the movement, crisscrossing flux toward the four corners of the square, finds himself walking in the direction of the Burg, raindrops, sweltering heat, a fresh shower.

Goes up on the sidewalk after the fountain, sees the pennants over there slipping into the wings, the banners with swastikas, sleight of hand, they'll be folded up, the tame joyless fair at an end, the stage empties out, rechristened a decade ago, already historic, Adolf-Hitler-Platz.

I'm surely not alone in wondering what happened, in being amazed, things moved so quickly, we weren't sufficiently on guard, things accelerated, lately, caught us up short, on the wrong foot, and with no recourse.

A crisis of something or other, of conscience, confidence, divergent analyses, contrary conclusions, this notion not particularly convincing. Or else a matter of pendulum swings, periods of flux, reflux, that wasn't it either.

A new event really, come without warning, unforeseen, intriguing, too extensive to be perceived by the doctors, the specialists, the computers, or to be retained in the polls, surveys, colloquiums, investigations.

If I say that I had a foreboding sometimes, evoked here and there, in veiled terms, in roundabout ways, what advantage today, what's the point.

Espoused its élan, at certain moments, its outcome supposedly fathomed, but it moved more quickly, didn't wait for the century's end, millennium balanced ahead of schedule and charged automatically to our account, sold off on the sly to settle all that could not be counted on, confirmed bankruptcy.

A statement of account from bygone years, disastrous, a celebrated continent shipwreck, everything was interlinked no doubt, arms, arts, hard to believe. Surely not alone in being amazed. But alone here in questioning, revisiting the places, the times, redealing the cards, wondering what happened, why, how.

Stumbling always on the same difficulties, insufficient, truncated clues, lack of proofs, unconfirmed pieces of information. A want of contradiction especially, of refutation. Alone here in turning things over, turning in circles, no more dialogue, not with the mere handful of poor creatures remaining in the village in spite of everything . . .

Withdrawn into the small house, comfortably settled in, more practical, bedroom, kitchen, living room, easy to manage as they say, housework quickly done, broom, dust cloths.

The dust outside the windows, on the nettles down below, the tall grass as far as the pond, the shimmering light on the water between the branches of the elms, the ashes, unimpeded view, as restful as one might want.

A setting that inspires meditation, eyes soothed, hardly anything to distract the gaze, meditate upon what, an absence of points of reference, of comparison, compare what, a far too new situation.

Disconcerting. Mustn't allow oneself to be completely drawn in, take a step back, a cool head, and respect a schedule: a walk in the morning, work in the afternoon, or vice versa, evenings for relaxation, TV or what's left of it, cassettes, play them while waiting.

Wrong time for nostalgia. To magnify the past, shed a tear over the good time so hard to live through back then, programmed inanity, fanciful sequels, ages since it doesn't click anymore.

To make do with the means at hand, improvise, for want of innovating, pragmatism in the place of honor, for once, eclectic choices, mustn't take offense, there have been situations like this before.

But no, that's just the point, never have people proved to be so inert, so mute, colorless, never so little news on the radio, slow-moving transports, if old Lambert hadn't restocked his shelves in June, a stroke of luck, what in God's name would we live on?

The feeling at times of a reiteration, resumption of a distant movement, someone might have lived this long ago, I might be in his trail, passing along in his footsteps without quite knowing, as if groping, resurgence of an ancient stage born by the collective unconscious or some completely different method of progression, backwash, an affront by history.

But that has its limits, immediate blockage, this kind of fiction is depressing, a better activity is observing things closely in the here and now, taking them as they come and treating them in my way, patiently bearing this difficulty, presuming it is one.

Eight in the evening, in the sunshine, no one spoke of adjusting the clocks this year, it's the time when I "move to the living room," raising the door curtain and entering the dark room across the creaking parquet.

The window here looks out on the pond, the view is more or less the same, save for the different angle allowing a glimpse between the trees of a somewhat vaster water surface, broader pale green beaches of aquatic vegetation which drifts slowly, or not at all when the level of the expanse settles below that of the wall downstream, I'll explain farther on, this is the case presently.

It has rained very little these first days of August, blue sky until noon, then an irruption of very slow cloud banks sailing from west to east over the *causse*, yellow and mauve at sunset, flushed pink, deep purple.

Fog often in the morning, blankety, I part the shutters and the work of nature, massively, opposes my expectation, thwarts my gaze already focusing on a distance, it's not the pond alone concealed from sight, the foliage also, the dirt path, the meadow.

In the evenings, fog occurs very rarely; in the evening it's a bad sign, say the people in these parts, a bad sign of what exactly isn't said. Ordinarily, a limpid atmosphere, milky vault of the sky, as if electrified, Mars glistening, shiny, a great tension between the figures.

I pull closed the shutters, leave the window open, turn on the set in the corner, it's time for the retrospectives, festivals of the years when signs were no doubt deteriorating, no one knew how to read them before it was too late, signs in the voices, music, ambivalent, deceptive.

I take the cassette from the shelf and push it into the recorder, Fortunate the power's on tonight, press the play button and go sit on the sofa in the opposite corner, rerun of an ancient displacement, following the trail, myself or another, reflux of history, how much time like this and who can tell where it will end, something else has begun perhaps.

The factory rises four floors along the train tracks running toward Mogeldorf, Lauf, red brick walls, somewhat timeworn, windows set high, the trains not in view and the sound of the machines sweeps him along, Martin riveted to his own, automated on the spot, in no time flat, left hand in an uninterrupted back-and-forth movement drawing the pieces from the tray, steel screws, and fastening them on the metal plate, right hand clenched on the lever activating the countersink bit, forward, back, pulling away his left hand in time, keeping up the pace, above all no slacking off, six thousand pieces a day.

Dizziness and cramps, in spells, eleven hours on his feet in front of the machine, Martin can't get over it, everything moved so quickly, grabbed after midnight by a patrol in his hometown and shipped here in no time, eighteen years old, student, didn't have time to breathe, it might've been worse after all, they must've made a mistake on some paper, gets off cheaply.

Assigned as unskilled labor, no apprenticeship, a foreman is called a meister here and a shop a section, the scant vocabulary salvaged from high school serves him, he shuts himself up in the lavatory with his German words.

German mastery, manpower from all nations, men and women, Russians, Ukrainians, Czechs and Serbs, Poles, from now on

Italians, the whole of Europe joining hands, central and eastern, a sheepish confluence, pathetic crucible, melting pot, Year Zero.

Those from the east wear the word "East" on their backs, white stencil on their coats stigmatizing the subwork force; a photo posted on the city walls shows three of their soldiers coming out of a wheat field hands in the air, worn out, alarmed, the caption reads: the subhuman.

The Ukrainian girls receive tiny packages, sachets of jute filled with sunflower seeds; they often sing in the shop, the high-pitched cries of their round dances obliterating almost instantly the rumbling of the motors.

The loudspeaker, the other morning, pouring forth music, broadcast an aria from *Carmen;* they took it up, spontaneously, they knew it by heart.

German women in the neighboring section, conscripted for arms manufacture, as all over everywhere, an intensified war effort, it's the factory or the front, if the front threatens collapse, the factory holds firm, no bomb has yet dropped on it, undamaged neighborhood in a nearby suburb, not far from the river, east of the city before the forest.

A few Frenchmen on the floor below, "freed" prisoners, adjusters, turners, talk little, keep to themselves, have been here for three years.

Men in black act as the police, black caps, old men, or unfit for service, circulate continuously in the hallways, the stairs, haunt the workshops at night where isolated lamps shine here and there over privileged machines whirring with no letup.

Closed off space in which the day unfolds, going in at six, coming out at six, every day consists in this solid obstacle passing slowly, opaquely, gaze fixed upon the point where the moving hands converge, a balance to be achieved between attentiveness and dropping off, precision and routine, carelessness, sudden starts, recalling instructions, lubricating the machine, checking calibers, every faulty item is added to the file, posted with no appeal, calculated in ells of peril.

Imputed sabotage and the workmates talk about it, the Germans first of all, quickly warned of the consequences: they cross their wrists in front of themselves for the edification of the neophytes, hands consigned to cuffs which more than one of them has experienced, gone off one day leaving no address behind; they say the name of the camp in a southern province, a sinister reputation, opened to receive them from the outset.

First German gesture learned, a mute gesture, unsubtitled, Martin recorded it right at the start, a word to the wise is enough, this gesture keeps running through his head, did they make it before, and what used to be manufactured here—before the events—toys, electric trains, dolls maybe, toy soldiers?

In this factory, before the war, were there policemen in black, and others in work-blue, in grey smocks, ears pricked up, noting everything in their heads and reporting every evening to the proper authority, so much gossip, tittle-tattle, idle babble, a rotten business, stool pigeon, how to avoid mixing everything up?

In this city before the war—he read it, he remembers—there was a strong party on the other side, an influential burgomaster, powerful unions, where are the militants, the men of law, the teachers from that time, where have they been for the past ten years?

Some are still working here perhaps, on file and under surveillance, detention camp hanging over them, and how to talk to them, who to talk to here except the Russians, joking with them during the breaks, at lunch they head toward a separate canteen, enforced segregation, imposition of decreed hierarchies, racial and national as well, the human pyramid crushed at its base, excessive outcome of centuries-long conflicts, bloody empires, deadly supremacies.

Sleepwalking continent, crippled, ravaged, drained of blood.

Eleven hours spent meditating before the steel tool and the mechanized traffic of factory-made pieces passing from left to right, from one hand to the other between the knives, piling up in the tray to the right where a cart comes to collect them, pushed by a mirthful Croatian guzzling the alcoholized liquid used for washing them.

Six o'clock, bell, commotion and a silence settles in, magical really, all the motors stop at the same time and Martin, numbed, beyond any meditation, mechanically cleans his machine, after showering he clocks out and passes through the gates between the men in black who frisk him sometimes.

Will follow the paved street, Stephenstrasse, his head heavy, legs and arms still trembling, as if made feverish by a persistent vibration, will move along the train tracks heading toward the center, before reaching the camp will turn into a narrow street to the right and climb onto the small bridge above the river, lean his elbows on the stone parapet.

Will look at the water a long while, the meadow on the other bank and the children at play.

Signs in the voices, the eyes, from another continent but they were speaking about our own, should have listened closer to Miles, seeing his hand again as it traces the ancestral African gesture of storyteller or sage sitting cross-legged, crouched in front of his door explaining the world, with a flick of his wrist his palm opening supremely skyward.

Complete leisure to watch him now, as long as the power lasts, replay the tape, his face wasted, the distant disdain, arm intuitively recapturing the subdued élan of Africa in the white America of managers and studios, down at the heels, yes, institutionalized along the way but so close to the margins.

He speaks haltingly, searches for his words, lowers his eyes and he seems to have lost the thread, tracking the mute discourse which secretly guides him, saps him, and then dubbing it with his hoarse voice, a husky prolongation of the sounds filtered by mouthpiece and mute.

Miles listened a lot, before playing, imitated a lot, polished formulas and clichés, only to clash them together, to short-circuit them, to distend, which only goes to prove that beauty is the brief burst inserted between two clichés: someone from his country said that, a cursed wartime poet.

Owl's screech in the darkness through the open window, I feel the summer breeze at night, recognizable rustling of the leaves, a branch cracks, falls into the water, the surface closes over it, darkness in the room and the small house beyond the zone of the screen where the past colors pass on a ghostly stature upon the musician, deepest purple, wide-sleeved jacket and blue-tinted seroual, whittled fingers, bare-domed forehead and long curly locks, hollowed pockmarked cheeks, and wide lips, a messenger come from afar bearing news, in rarefied notes, strident staccato attacks and moist muffled sounds, slipping past tonality through a touch of tongue and valves prowling under the player's splayed phalanx.

Black inquiring eyes, not piercing, but insistent, imperious at times, ironic upstream, then averted, lowered, taming the note to come, masked by the large smoky rectangular lenses.

One finger, two fingers, three fingers set on the neck, the cheek, the forehead, pressing deeply, pushing the skin on the upper cheekbones, smoothing it under the eye as if questioning the skin, the circulation, taking blood pressure.

Bowing, leaning very far forward, gathering his strength, knees bent, releasing the notes as if from his whole body this way, from top to bottom, voice cast earthward.

Ruminating lips, chewing his lips, gums, teeth, sticking together, absorbing the wait, molding the vehemence of the phrasing, the distance covered very daring, innovative, what was done six months ago can't be repeated, he says, pushed toward what, knowing that one must never stop, seek, never be satisfied, never imitate oneself, whoever does so perishes, repudiates himself, disappears.

Lunar happening, disarming, mechanism set in motion and inventing its road, machine that switches things around, varies, for as long as the sorcerer doesn't raise his arm to stop it with one flick, gaze slightly uncertain when he relifts his head, releasing his instrument, but still absorbed, riveted on the élan, unsure of himself perhaps but sure of the élan, the quality of the élan, of its necessity.

Tape come to an end, I rewind and they draw back up in proper order, he and his kindred souls, those from the forties, fifties, they had faith in an idea, all forms must change, differ from themselves at a certain point and sound otherwise, a law of nature, they followed it, it was taken for granted all in all, that the élan would endure, the player's élan, the city's, that the player would be accepted, have rights to the city, that the city wouldn't die, who killed it then, see it all again, play other tapes.

I put the cassette back in its cabinet beside the books, a long while since I've read the books, the élan in the eyes and hand of the crouched man explaining his life dismisses the silence again, I remain seated while the last tempo beats, regulating the heart's own beating, more than once I slept here looking at the glow around the outer edge of the shutters.

But usually I leave my living room and its wonders in darkness, a luxury in times such as these, and lifting the curtain recross the threshold, in the short hallway unbolt the door and plant myself outside feet in the grass, focusing very quickly on the meadow on the other side of the dirt path and the oaks of the *causse,* in moonlight the stones of the *causse* stand out with a dull gleam in the night and I often went walking there, just a few months ago, smoking a pipe, but tobacco, alcohol have become currency, I keep my hands off, learn to walk without smoking a pipe.

For a while also I haven't been afraid, feel at ease here, too many objects in the big house, furniture, stairs, shadow recesses, too many worries, the old Perret woman gone off, too many concerns, here I've never been afraid, no more midnight alarms.

I shut the door all the same, never can tell, if a noise awakens me it's made by a mouse in the attic, a clear reassuring progress, or by the rain, been ages since any cars have gone by on the road, no gasoline, never comes up on the radio, silence.

These things never come up, too vast a period, century scale, not taken into account and who notices them, faster than first thought, they die out.

Questions without answers, and then, no more questions.

It used to be the Fine Arts School, the phosphorus tracers burned the roofs, the pinnacles, two floors under the roofs, Martin found a photo in a pile of rubble, page torn from a book, the building shown in its entirety, before the war, in the twenties no doubt, an open tourer parked before the entrance attests this, edifice in pink sandstone, massive, end of century, a barracks or charmless high school.

The two remaining floors, ground floor, cellars, make up the camp; have become the foreigners' camp, all nations mixed together, in the random order of conquests, conscripted manpower, evacuations and raids, bombings, relocations. No trace of the paintings, easels, pedestals, brushes, but plaster molds in the hallways and recesses, enormous heads of gods, of philosophers, orators, pallidly stationed right on the floor tiles, haunting the walls, or in the courtyard emerging wanly from the ashen vestiges of the beams and stones.

The study halls emptied of all antique content, housing nothing more than wooden bunk beds, a dozen per room, a table in the middle and wooden closets, the blue-tinted bay windows allowing in a dull, shadowy, uneven light.

Martin in the slow-moving train exiling him in midsummer, destined for Central Europe, hadn't imagined a camp in the middle of town, so close to an old city, to the Ring, its ramparts, nineteenth-century camp next to a town from the Middle Ages renowned for its culture and history.

He has been there for two months and more, every evening, very tired, third floor, enters the barracks on the street side where the others have already come back, Czech workers from

Prague, French peasants from the western regions, still dumb-founded, no wine, no tobacco, remaining there in the evening, talking homeland, disconcerted.

They can go out, until eleven, don't do so, don't speak the language, don't care to, or dare not. Those marked "East," on the courtyard side, don't have this right; confined there, they can be heard singing at times, on the other side of the wooden partitions dividing the hallways on each floor.

Policemen in black also, visible especially at night, keep watch at the entrances, exits, respect for camouflage, proper order in the barracks. Alsatian interpreter, Sudeten camp commander and his wife reside in three comfortably furnished rooms, bourgeois, or rather very petit-bourgeois, they aren't members of the elite, and it's wartime.

If he stretches out on his straw mattress, Martin falls asleep, still in his clothes, and without eating. Then, he leaves, puts on a tie and goes out in the coat he bartered for cigarettes exchanged at a loss against bread coupons.

Goes back up Marienstrasse in the mist, October has arrived, the frost, dazed, headachy, has the impression he was already going back up Marienstrasse in his childhood, would go back up his eyes closed at present and would cross the Ring, the trolleys stretch into the distance, so few cars, would reopen them at Marientor where the roadway narrows, slippery cobblestones and poor visibility, blue-tinted streetlamps in the fog, extremely steep roofs and gables on the medieval street, somewhat deserted, a small wan lamp above a porchway and it's the fish restaurant where he sometimes comes, orders a breaded cutlet, a beer, ersatz cream and goes out again into the night, warmed up a bit, forgets the factory.

Eight o'clock, going to take a walk, it's the second part of the day, the other panel, goes down toward the river, discovers or re-discovers the small streets, without a map but no risk of getting lost, plentiful landmarks, natural, cultural.

The river is the surveyor's staff, privileged vector, east-west, determining the symmetrical slopes and declivities of the city within its diamond-shaped surrounding walls marked by towers and ditches.

He passes the river on Museumsbrücke, crosses the main square, not crowded, scattered milky lights, then the incline becomes appreciable nearing the hill to the north and something happens inside him, he reaches the theater, there's the stage, he finds it again, the scene of his readings, recaptures what he's read, looked at, listened to, what he knew about this country when he was fifteen, used to read this country's books, the tales, stories, formed his own personal idea about it, the idea persists in spite of everything, in spite of what the war has taught him, he forgets the war upon passing the bridge, he's on the other side of the bridge, the ghosts come to meet him, melodies and songs, myths, novels, mad dashes through the white forest, Burg soon in sight between the fantastical trunks, clouds sinisterly swift upon the skylights, the sharp angles of the house frames and the flowered balconies.

Here are found the names for restoring the aura, restoring it romantically, the names that once composed this country's marvelous image, knights out of magic, Gothic engravers and makers of stringed instruments, philosopher-kings, musicians of language and writers of sounds.

The other evening at the same time, backtracking near Tiergärtnertor, he raised his eyes and saw that he was on Albrecht-Dürer-Strasse, going down toward the river, and he stopped, reread the inscription and an instant later the sirens sounded, immediately afterward the night planes arrived, the defense searchlights formed something like a moving dome of light, broken, scored sheaves in which the machines glimmered, drawing the stunned gaze and holding it captive in the upper regions of the picture.

Bombs fell, on a southern suburb, he saw the flashes, then a red glow rose, revealing the clouds in the background, on the horizon composing a vaguely defined, menacing, pallid plume.

Waking up as in the past, the room looked out on the orchard, I used to go down the timeworn stairs and open the house wide, this was before the incidents, people still talked, discussed, grew animated, there was still food for controversy.

Obsolete frame of mind, upon waking I find myself in it at times, old reflex, then I open the window and see the pond, the large house over there on the other side of the pond, everything comes back to me this very second, the loss of interconnections, this atony, no more contact.

An absence of something being at stake, and perhaps even more: of the consciousness of something at stake—age-old, it used to be said, consubstantial with this country, this civilization—consciousness of its necessity, of its power. A glaring absence, made commonplace, grown used to by all around, flat horizon, everything falls back into place at first glance and I walk into the adjoining room, fix tea, I've got a good supply of tea, sugar, coffee.

Kitchen supplies here, between bedroom and living room, multipurpose space, also including toiletries, the practical essentials on a three-meter-long shelf, autonomous unity, to be kept up, replenished.

Everything needed for washing up, soap, brushes, towels. Shaving, no, out of blades, beard not very becoming, pepper and salt, uneven. I cut my own hair from time to time, big scissor-clips in the three-sided mirror.

No telephone, I left it over there, wasn't working anymore, hours of waiting, no mail either, weeks at a time, nothing to communicate but still . . .

I go to the village twice a week, a small village, city hall, church and post office on the square across from the large linden, the narrow street where the butcher's and baker's stand opposite each other, old Lambert a little farther on, his grocery can be made out as you pass in front, no sign anymore.

The war memorial is at the end of the street, right after the bistro, thirty-two dead for three wars, names engraved in the stone, an obsessive roll call of honor in the paradise of the brave, heavy catalogue, three massacres for a decline.

I stop and circle the monument, at the foot of the hill, have only one brake, basket on the luggage rack, get off and leave the bike in front of the door, bell, old Lambert is rocking in his chair, cap over brows, cigarette in mouth.

Repeats the same things all the time, recent departures, soon nobody at the train going wherever, as if there weren't enough unemployed people in town, they move off westward, northward, utopic, he says, meaning mythic no doubt.

Walks into the back of the store, returns with my cans, peas, beans, lentils, pasta, rice; a bottle of olive oil, his surprise of the month, a special flavor, no more butter for some time.

Two packs of Gitanes in return for this good favor, he slips them into his hiding place, what will I do when I'm all out, a rich idea the other year, ought to have stocked up even more, and some tobacco too, pastis, whiskey, even more, who might have imagined.

My last time out, for all that, the old Ford up to the mark through the snow, a back tire blown, no more spares, the car on blocks since then, in the garage under the small house.

The woman at the bakery, gone to seed behind her counter, reappeared the other week to the neighbors' surprise, slips me some eggs for once, joins them to the large round loaf of bread. Butcher absent, back on Monday they say, isn't there often anymore, the deaf old man, meat stall empty for some time.

I push on to the post office. Mailman retired, not replaced, but Madame Paule still present, faithful to her mission, a stable element, hasn't all that much to do anymore but surprises happen, it's good she's at her task, receiver within hand's reach, printed forms, phone books and stamps, seeing her in her tiny office is reassuring.

Shows me a newspaper come the day before, a daily dated July

20, no headlines, the crisis, a summit meeting, grave tension in the southwest, sports take up all the rest, fashions, sales, recipes, how to spend a nice vacation at home.

Trash, she says, who'd have thought this just one year ago, you'd think they're doing it on purpose, the press, really, everything's going to the dogs, does it make any sense to you?

None, I shrug, if that was the only problem. Get back on my bike, check the basket, pass by the monument again and turn onto the small road to go back, the tennis court being overrun by dandelions, the cave where people lined up back at the height of summer, then the dirt path through the woods, barely outlined now, the antique *caselle* under the thistles and at the bend afterwards, the meadow in sight, the path meeting marked by the cross, the tile roof, pedaling a little more, coasting along the last stretch.

In a sweat, leaden sky this morning, the grass turning brown, a good shower will do the trick. At the crossroad, there, two paths in the meadows, I should be seeing, right in front of me, the farm on the other slope of the valley, disappearing under the bushes at present, we often went walking there, the big dog sprang out from behind the shed, escorting us up to the tobacco fields, turning around and barking, then growing weary, backtracking and allowing us to continue in peace.

We'd go as far as La Plane sometimes, we were all there at that time, the summer months, at Christmas too some years, braving the frost, stoking the vast fireplace with logs in the large room below, talking about our projects, our current work, something would be going on, each week, each day, there was a general movement, a general élan, appearing quite natural.

Those times seem far-off, difficult to place, after the war certainly, but a bygone era, as if carried out on another star. Memory negates chronology, updates and distorts, I'm imagining things maybe, excessively embellishing, comparisons would need to be made, between memories and areas of knowledge, but with whom, I wonder.

And the memory of these moments, in this time of isolation, of futility, of emptiness, what will it be later on? Will it also betray, deceive?

Will embellish, no doubt.

And these times will be the good old days.

The ceiling bulb comes on, five o'clock, this he knows right off, while it's happening, Martin, one of those whom the least flicker, the least sound awakens, hears the cop in black climbing the stairs, banging with his fist on the doors.

Bombs on this area of the city at the end of October and the school got knocked around one more time, split ceilings, snow comes in through the cracks, Martin throws back his blanket and a dust of flakes falls on the tiles, sharp cold, blades of straw in his hair, bounds out of bed, obligatory exercise, jumps from the second rung to the edge of the first, regains his balance and dashes to the shower room in the hallway corner, splashes on some icy water, shaves, when the painters and sculptors were around they washed colors here no doubt, plaster, sizing.

Then dashes across the cobblestones through the darkness, stumbling, nothing but the sound of his footsteps, his stumbling, everybody mute, dozing, sidewalks piled with crumbled stones, snow-covered beams, rubble, passes under the trestle after Bahnhofstrasse and goes up along the tracks, factory in sight, its red-tiled pinnacles, crosses through the gates and clocks in, nightmare at dawn, he won't come out again for twelve hours or more.

Surprise one beautiful morning, the foreman removes him from his machine, another he's never seen before sticks him in the courtyard in front of a cart, and now ever since he's been pushing the cart with no letup, lugging packing cases into the elevators and hallways, from the warehouses to the workshops, from the workshops to the cellars, bringing, taking, going down, up, circulating from morning to night, in his own way.

He tells himself it's better this way, he was given clogs, he's moving at least, barefooted in the clogs, perhaps he'll finally find out what's being manufactured in this factory, among all the parts ferried around until now no two fit together, they must be assembled elsewhere, in a related factory, on the other side of the city perhaps, on the other side of the country?

After several days of performing these duties, methodically exploring each floor, pushing open all the doors, sequentially trying paths and circuits, he knows almost every recess of the buildings. What's essential is always to be transporting some object, looking busy, ready with an explanation for any question from a supervisor or policeman suddenly wondering at his presence in an isolated or unlikely place.

His itinerant status furnishing him very naturally with numerous pretexts for exchanging a few words along his way with the sedentary workers, who ask for nothing better, if not to converse even longer, more regularly. With some among them, he thus manages to spend days a little less maddening than the ones on his feet in front of his machine, even gathering bits of information on occasions.

Learning a few words of Russian, Ukrainian, Italian, with the prisoners in torn uniforms who speak distressfully of their city in the north on the front lines, left without food after the camp guards arrived, forced by them to beg, to enter the barracks on their knees, hands out for some bread.

Noticing that the number of this country's male and female citizens working in the factory is much greater than he thought. Mobilized here, and in other factories, young and old, the necessities of war, able-bodied girls and women, and men rejected for military service, handicapped, everyone conscripted, the maimed and hunchbacked, those injured in the other war.

He received a shock, last week, reaching the fifth floor in the southern wing, which he had somewhat neglected until then, pushing open the elevator door and discovering a very long narrow workshop under the roof, at the threshold of which, at first glance, something unusual stopped him.

Silence. No machines, and nobody talking along the two rows of men seated on either side of an enormous table, fifty or so men checking the uniformity of the manufactured parts, gauge in hand, after inspection decanting them from one box to the other, and nothing but the multiplied tinkling of the metal objects, a diffuse rustling, uninterrupted, filling the premises.

Taken aback, Martin observes the mute workers stationed face to face in the poorly lit workshop, the skylights in the roof allowing only a dim glow to filter in. Then drawing near, notices that they are looking straight ahead, heads erect, don't look at their hands moving very rapidly as if self-driven, mechanically, don't look at anything, the men are blind.

He remains fixed to the spot, in disbelief, and two of the men, those closest, turn their heads toward him, without slowing down the back-and-forth motion of their hands, without saying a word, turn their eyes toward him.

Martin withdrew, noiselessly, went back to the elevator, closed the door and stayed there a moment without thinking to go down, thought that those men in the shadows were checking weapons, shell parts no doubt, validating them with their hands, bomb parts that were soon going to explode, that were going to pierce and to mutilate, to burn hands, eyes, to blind, to lacerate, one generation of the blind mutilating the next, blinding them, from one war to the next, from one new process of mutilation to the next, a technique of blinding, of subjection, hands always moving back and forth, mechanically, without recourse, without end.

He spoke to no one in the workshop of the blind. Doesn't know why, dreads perhaps that hearing this, someone would break out laughing.

Or snickering: this is what they're reduced to.

As if the war here mobilized only the blind.

I think I've solved all my problems, meaning the practical ones, those posed by these new disconcerting circumstances, all except for the flies. No more flypaper, of course; I tried vinegar, unsuccessfully. They're swarming in the kitchen, in the bedroom too, the living room, choosing beams of sunlight, settling on every lit surface, seemingly drawn by some likelihood of booty.

Ninety-four degrees, heavier these last few days, typical of August when the air stagnates, a ceiling fan would make things better, but we're not in the tropics.

Often I set up the garden table in front of the door on the small terrace overhanging the water cistern, but today it's even more stifling than inside and I confine myself to the kitchen, beating my eggs, preparing the frying pan, now and then, for peace of mind, waving the fan brought back from Malaysia in better days, whose green and yellow palm threads, finely woven in groups of symmetrical figures, infallibly make the patient recall the dominant colors of a jungle landscape where it's even hotter and more humid. And they don't just have flies over there, for stinging the skin, or lizards for slipping under stones.

I congratulated myself, running about the temples, plagued by mosquitoes, on being in a temperate country, wondering how, under such a relentless sky, such sweltering heat, such a continual bath of sweat, anybody at all could still argue ideas, discuss business or politics, write or read, or simply think.

But I really liked those distant incursions, no matter how brief, which allowed at last the place of origin to be isolated, through its difference in a way, to be delineated, identified, introducing novel perspectives by the sole fact of changing latitude and climate, changing angle of vision if such may be said, angle of reflection. This relativization of viewpoints was precious for us, a recycling rather, in a good many ways, it diversified our voices.

Periods of travel, after the war, of discoveries, other languages and continents, other networks of history, kinds of customs and of economies, other beliefs, values, ways of praying, feeling, narrating. Everything the war had blocked off, fatally regressive,

Europe clenched to its failings, its self-sufficiency and contempt, its special gifts of blindness, its secret vow of consumption and bankruptcy.

The time between the two wars, do you remember, troubled betweentime of adolescence, they talked only about them, in the press, at home, the one that had just ended, the one that was going to come, definitely break out, one fine morning, and to disperse, set fire, terrify, wound.

To undermine the child and its games, scoff at the stories of the elders, to foreclose the meager knowledge in books. Convulsed period of the past, interwoven with parades, coups d'état, great convoys on land and through air, in the tales, the voices—and everything that wasn't known, that was being perpetrated on the other battle's slope, hidden by it, in the shadows and the mud, nullifying centuries of enlightenment.

Mourning for history, comes back often, to explain what follows, at high noon, a day like today, recorded once and for all, not only in pictures, one-eyed films striped with grey, but on the tape inside the head, endlessly turning, indelible, wearing oneself out by scratching in vain, to erase the marks, rerecord something more lighthearted, more lively, a cool playback against a background of flames.

Virgin cassette of the child, flecked with black.

At this point, unhook, cut the antenna, no point in listening to voices anymore, there're better things to do, scrutinize the surrounding area and take note, fortify the small island, not to let oneself be overcome by torpor, that overall drowsiness, that inertia, mental languor, an unnamed insect has stung men's brains, exotic bumblebee, to protect oneself at all costs.

Indifferent ritual of lunch, no surprises, bland canned vegetables, no more cheeses, the orchard's cherry plums whittled away by wasps, sucked in, sucked dry.

At coffee time I go out onto the terrace, a matter of principle, and linger upon the garden chair a while sipping the timely beverage, recapitulating, flapping the fan, taking bearings.

The clouds have amassed above the valley, barely shifting, sweltering heat here below as if the echo of a furnace.

At the foot of the terrace invaded by weeds and thistles begins the sloping footpath that leads to the dirt road, a country lane for two hundred yards until reaching the cracked surface of the departmental road, indented with potholes, and its two lanes, climbing toward the village on the right, cutting through the *causse*, and to the left across fields and pastures, connecting several deserted hamlets last year where lethargic dogs camp out, keeping watch as over a treasure.

I go for a stroll out that way, from time to time, just "to see," but there's nothing much to see, I'm talking about human beings, not before Pradelle at any rate, more than two leagues away. At many sites, nature has reclaimed its rights, and this cliché the utmost topicality.

Strange, pedaling along this road, alone, absolutely certain that no one will overtake me, or that, after a sharp curve, I'll come smack upon a harvester or tipcart.

Population drain of the farmland, people said in the past. Now, everything seems to be obeying a well-defined movement, of vast magnitude, no one able to clarify its end point, or cause.

But what good pandering to this idea, a malignant temptation. No project anywhere, no program, no reason of state; nothing well-defined in this matter, if not a grand passivity, depression, abandonment.

Danger, here, on my chair, vaguely contemplating the stones, copses.

Let's go, up on your feet, off to work.

Now winter's come, Christmas soon, Martin didn't believe it. Didn't believe he'd have to spend the winter here, didn't expect to.

Retreat in the east, threats in the west, cowardice of the Latin ally, the war would soon be over, the European fortress surrounded, taken by assault, fronts broken through before year's end.

Nothing of the sort, much to the contrary, the fervor has intensified, a very clear resolve, and the night raids exasperate, no question of giving way, even less of surrendering, the speeches attest to it, proclamations, slogans.

Martin reads the evening newspaper, deciphers the press releases, learned to decode them, cryptic military staff language, falling back in hedgehog formation, elastic defense. It's a withdrawal, but step by step, so they let it be understood, only to pounce forward all the better.

While waiting, the cold is severe, and the frost, the air-raid sirens multiply, the clear rumbling of the bombers catches the sirens short sometimes, flushes out the sleepers. Racing down the stairs, the shelters' armored doors close heavily upon the stunned visitors in the blackness.

Ears pricked up, seem to anticipate the racket, for a chance to cushion the shock, short-lived ruse, on the alert for what's taking place up above, at ground level and in the air, wrongly interpreting the dull thuds.

Oppressive silence in the stifling, stinking premises, but the radio suddenly transmits, a faraway neutral voice, simply sounding preoccupied, the voice of a technician, with a view of the big picture, better sheltered no doubt.

The same sentences every time, limited laconic repertoire, large enemy squadrons are approaching our city, lying in wait, heavily counting off the seconds and the eternal beating.

Waiting, steady noise of the planes under the cloud ceiling, sharp crack of the defense guns, no explosions making the earth tremble, so then tonight won't be the night, they've passed by, have gone to drop their bombs elsewhere.

The voice confirms that the danger has moved off, sleep comes again, smells of tar, paint, overheated cast iron in the jam-packed recess, hermetically sealed, how much longer still, slow suffocation, bouts of nausea, then a sudden start, the voice stirs, other formations have been reported, fast approaching, and the obsessive count starts over again, deadly.

Several times like this, one hour, hours on end, stomach heaves, they refrain from breathing the confined fetid air. At a certain point, badly situated, the voice from elsewhere, overcoming torpor, seemingly alone in still keeping watch, drops the words, the end of the emergency is announced, bustle, the steel door opens again, continuous sirens, fresh air in the hallway, up above, black night.

Several nights in a row this way, sleep broken, gone by the wayside, sleepwalking factory days. Evenings Martin goes for a walk despite everything, a matter of principle, giving his muscles free play and the disconcerting, now familiar spectacle, shop windows half sunk in the darkness, the almost secret entrance in Plärrer to a movie house under the pale lamplight.

Survival in halftones, at night, of the city, as if hushed, padded in the snow, rare pedestrians, rare cars, each hastens toward a precise goal, no stopping on the sidewalks, no conversations, no verbal exchanges, are out of place now, strange appearance of a city that seems submerged in the shadows, inhabited by silent people, absorbed, stingy with gestures and projects, passing along without lingering from one spectral zone to another, where the light is parsimonious, respected, sanctioned.

Across the whole of Europe, he muses, more or less across every city and every village of Europe, blue-tinted windows, telltale glimmers, curfew. Epoch of waning daylight, of night within the darkness of night, each has done his part to get to this point, fatal sequence, it all happened very quickly, two decades, from sidestepping to concessions, botched agreements, treasons, denials, double-dealing.

Fascination with force, sought out today, on what face can it still be found, in what gait across the broken cobblestones, blind, as if following its own momentum, uncontrolled, with no return.

Tripping over rubble, furtive glance skyward, dreading the stars.

He gets back to the camp before ten, the others already snoring, collapses on his straw mattress, clothes within hand's reach.

In his sleep hears the sirens a hundred times, slinking along the walls, is stopped by a night-light level with his forehead, allowing him to make out a flight of steps. He walks down, and at the very bottom stumbles upon the river.

An image on a screen.

The large elms are dying, I cut down three last year, killed by graphiosis, death by suffocation, the microscopic mushroom blocks the sap ducts.

The two left by the pond's shore, I have them in view every time I raise my eyes, and the ashes farther left, very near the water. I also see a triangle of water, and the branches of the plane tree on the other bank.

No matter how long I've dawdled on the terrace after lunch, or in the kitchen putting away the food, putting off the ever-nearing deadline, the moment always comes, most often unawares, when I find myself again in front of this table, pencil in hand, surrounded by all these papers, and at that point, I really wonder why.

A momentum of its own, if one likes, but come from another age. When this kind of work still had meaning, strictly speaking, back in that age, the question could still be asked. Whereas, now . . . But it's stronger than I, the force of a tradition perhaps, or the inability to break with it.

Or the idea that there is something to maintain, despite everything, something to transmit, even if it's not much at all, who will decide? Somebody will stumble upon it one far-off day, will decipher, become amazed, say how curious, it was unexpected, people still wrote at the end of the twentieth.

A piece of moldy paper, practically illegible, found in a cupboard between two piles of worm-eaten files having miraculously escaped disinfection. Or else scorched, half turned to ash, surviving an explosion or a great high altitude flash.

A manner of milestone, road marker, to verify that someone

passed that way, on that day, that he thought this, and wrote it down, no matter how stupid, the person finding it will perhaps give me a thought, it's not out of the question after all, I'd really like to know what sort.

But I don't think that's it either, no matter how reassuring the perspective may appear. Even if someone swore to me, backed with proof, that everything here within a given radius will be annihilated in the near future, I would still continue all the same, and therein lies the mystery.

The frenzy of some people, upon spotting a blank sheet, at the idea it might stay untouched. And scribbling away. But it's not in order to bear witness, or leave a mark, what's the point, but rather to focus one's faculties perhaps, mobilize body and mind, balance the day, at one chosen moment, the world, at one chosen moment of the day, of the world.

No antecedent among my ancestors, no future with things as they are, a little bit each day, not a novel, God spare me, nor an essay nor a lampoon, but the very play that the radio people asked from me several years ago, even commissioned from me, I signed the contract, and that's where matters stood, for their part.

But I worked on it. The fact that the station has long since broken off transmissions isn't enough to stop me, as mentioned above. Culture fallen in disrepute, it was to be expected, at the rate things were going. No more news, nothing surprising, any they might give would get lost in the mail.

But it's not inconceivable that communications be reestablished one of these days, progressively, in a distant future of course, given the current state of deterioration. This crisis not sensed by the soothsayers, poorly described, latent, will indeed evolve in one direction or another after all, and I'll be ready, text in hand, I got an advance as well, I'm duty-bound to honor it.

But that's not it, once again, I would work on it at any rate, advance or not, polish my dialogues. I started off with a rather simple idea, a woman comes in to record her voice, an organization exists for that expressed purpose, the scientific study of voice characteristics, attesting to them, delivering a piece of paper as proof which holds currency in commercial circulation, in the audiovisual sector for example, since it's radio.

The young woman enters the studio, her surprise in front of the host of microphones, high-spirited beginning, snappy exchanges, it was during the other winter, there still were contacts then, it didn't occur to anyone that things would keep getting worse, the analyzing machine functioned wonderfully, the applicant articulated to perfection, numerous takes were made, it was last year that the instruments went haywire, one after another, jammed, dialogues come to a standstill.

I had to start over again from the very beginning, look for what wasn't right, the point where things weren't right anymore, arduous task, at times it was necessary to go back very far, an overlong sentence here, too short there, an innocuous-looking word creates static in the text and the tone drops, the intensity slackens, the whole thing crumbles.

On some afternoons, I feel in top form, no disturbances, ideas come flooding; on others, like today, the weather interferes, the uncomfortable heat, difficult to weigh carefully each nuance when sweat is streaming, bathing one's face, hands; flies and mosquitoes landing every second on the paper, distracting my eyes, coming to suck and sting the skin.

Doors and windows wide open, poised for a cool draft, but nothing, the sky is cloudy again, a rumble in the west, distant storm; here, still no rain.

Elements in suspense, air and plant, birds mute with torpor, dry grass and tarnished leaves of the enormous trees before me, drooping, crumbling away, bare upper branches, the mushroom is working away, for decades no doubt, cases were reported before the war.

I'll cut down those as well, incomparable heating wood for this winter, plant willows in their place, ashes, plane trees, chestnuts, along the edges of the pond, all along the brook upstream.

In the water, bald cypresses.

Ceaseless recycling of cells, prolific, age-old relay, fibers and nerves, roots. Humus—brown soil, blackish, on the earth's surface.

The most perverse defoliants waste away there.

On the enormous esplanade, the flagstones are pulling free, the grass has invaded everything, weeds, thistles. On the rows of steps demarcating the vast quadrilateral, the stones have come apart and, breaking the alignment, hang askew, precariously balanced, and the weeds, there also, have filled the gaps, along with moss, couch grass.

The tribune is intact, aside from the watermarks, but the large laurel-ringed swastika in concrete dominating the complex is half in ruins, hit by a rocket. One of the two monumental bronze eagles has disappeared, the masts of honor are smashed.

There is a feeling of total abandon, this place is left to its fate, other theaters of operation have supplanted it for several summers, the men convoked there each year for the grandiose rituals, those in black caps wielding shovels, then those in steel helmets bearing rifles and submachine guns, have had every opportunity to stream westward, eastward, southward as far as the Nile almost and the Caspian, have returned, beating a retreat, slowly approaching their point of departure, backwards, step by step, this defeated parade ground, site of fanatical harangues, that astounded and fascinated the world.

Seated on the uneven soiled steps of Luitpoldarena, contemplating the mournful deserted site, Martin fails to picture in imagination the assemblies of the past. Yet, the images are in his memory, photographs and newsreels, it's not so old, those mise-en-scènes, those pagan organizations of congresses where each institution had its day, party, army, platoon, youth. The apotheosis was played out on the seventh evening under the dome of light, where the leader advanced alone, and through the power of the showman's sound and light spectacle on a colossal scale, this man, so nondescript in appearance, wound up virtually deified on the spot due to the great space and drums.

These performances were the exact opposite of the *kammerspiel*. It seems to him that a century has elapsed between the overflowing faithful and the vacant field, the whole complex empty today, so little time calendarwise, four, five years, but the two spectacles remain mutually exclusive, irreconcilable, one springs from the other however, the liberated strength has been depleted in the four corners of Europe and the water, air, and plant kingdom have regained the upper hand.

This isn't the first time Martin has come here on Sundays, haunts these grounds, this place intrigues him, the shock and disturbance that was plotted here, the aggressions, treasons, the war and what followed, the ruin of his country, the revenge of the seditious, the mystification mounted upon a prestigious name.

The crumbling of innate values, jamming of ideas, his schooling foundered there and his childhood readings, everything he'd learned and saw trampled, doctored, travestied. It happened right here, this undermining of history, elsewhere as well, in minds, this shameless tampering, it was hidden from him, until the task was accomplished.

The patent dilapidation of the high place of debauchery is right there under his eyes, rather than under the rubble in the city, the bombs are not to blame here, but rather the force of circumstances in a way, the staggering drain of people from these gigantic requisite terrains: palace and parade ground, large German stadium, triumphal way were supposed to be erected as far as the eye could see along a grandiose axis, imperial Burg as focal point, over there on its hill, guarantee of antique glory, medieval alibi.

The enclosed green within the track turned to scrub and thorny bushes around the pond, Dutzendteich, where town dwellers go boating, pushing their oars through the polluted water. Suburb of empty lots, isolated huts, rickety fences, then come fallow fields, and continuing along the dirt paths, one soon reaches the large forest to the east, Lorenzerwald, its well-marked lanes, radiating intersections, pines standing in rows in the sandy soil and under-growth of bracken, mythological woodland.

To go up into the forest and come down into the other valley to the north, return at night by train, how to convince those back in the barracks, they stay behind on Sundays sleeping and playing cards, writing letters, talking homeland.

Martin wrote home twice, received a letter after many weeks, several lines censored, crossed out in black, then nothing more, doesn't know if he ought to write again.

A spell of mild weather these past days, the snow is melting, no air-raid alarms for three weeks now, the north is targeted as the year begins. Martin splashes through the mud, crosses the espla-nade, circles the pond, comes back toward the trolley station.

In Galgenhof he sees a movie house, goes down, and without looking at the poster buys his ticket, settles in the dark, the news-reels are on, the latest from the front in the ice and snow on the plains out there where cannons and tanks maneuver in slow motion under the gusts of flurries.

Then a comedy, fairly new, patterned after Hollywood, frivo-lous thirties-style banter, timid gags and syrupy refrains, film production hasn't run dry of these peacetime distractions, as if nothing had happened, a person could let himself be lulled if the colors weren't so ugly.

People scattered around the seats, old women, a few girls who feel like dancing, but dancing is forbidden in the rare cafés that have music. Perhaps they've never danced once yet. And the children, never really played, those who are three, four.

Adults, the game masters—here, elsewhere—annihilators full of envy, vicious wreckers.

Hardened veterans of the game, those who have perverted the rules.

I've said "pond," referring to an ornamental body of water, most often running, except in the summer, when reduced to a few puddles upon the hardened, brownish clay, cracked along narrow irregular paving stones, very jagged, strewn with twigs.

Some summers, there is no water left at all, the stream runs dry, I take advantage of this to unblock the fence where branches lodge all year long, large stones, compact heaps of dead leaves.

This year, a rather long pool subsists, not reaching the fence however, and since it's shallow, with the passing days a greyish, bluish film glazes the stagnating liquid, streaked with an iridescent yellow and silver.

It's the site of a geological leakage, the stream's water flows into a limestone fissure and disappears from sight, comes out again twelve miles or so to the west, certified by the flow of dyes, a distant resurgence allows the imagination to picture a tortuous route traced out in reaches and sheets of water and streaming confluences within the darkness below.

The natural site was laid out at the start of the last century, redesigned, filled in, a balancing reservoir constructed in case of floods, a vaulted tunnel forming a sump, this time of year a few steps take you down, once the fence is removed. I ventured there sometimes, running the beam of the flashlight over the already dry walls, upon the platform at the very bottom, the narrow mouth piercing the rock and the slanting conduit sinking underground, polished by time.

Moving into the blackness, hollowing its hole, its way drop by drop along the mineral cleavages and erosion, accumulating in sealed cavities until, dissolving a chalky vein, it allows the flow through, a traveled distance made up of detours and dead ends, diversions, digressions and backtracking, beyond any mapping, beyond sketches and drawings, unsuspected in its meanderings and sudden complication upon contact with ancient strata or chance objects, fossil or reptile forest from another age, but relentlessly winding about, physically, chemically, taking its time, lingering in the depths of caves until overflowing and escaping in a waterfall.

Unperceived trickle, enduring, tenacious along its slope, running lost, surreptitiously, with the potential for a new gushing, a new manifestation in daylight, at an unexpected moment, an always surprising place, forgotten.

Those who see it spring up don't know it's reborn, have no inkling of its underground trip, even less of the point where it veered into the earth's folds, burrowed down and slinked along, inaugurated its temporary passage through the shadows.

Once amazement passes, those who see it vanish from the surface give little thought to its fate, short-lived memory, there is no transmission of observations, verification of data, there's too much to do with what can be heard, what is manifest, present, and no doubt things are fine that way.

The burying place takes on a strange look in extreme cases, run dry or flooded, startling landscapes, unrecognizable, all landmarks altered, curves, surface details, colors.

Many winters ago it rained so much that, in time, inner chamber, balancing reservoir and streambed having duly filled up, the water overflowed the perimeters and spread across the banks, rising very high until covering the grass between the two houses, then reaching the walls of the large building, almost encircling it.

A unique fact in local history. I took snapshots, drew the contours of the shimmering spectacle.

It was the year of the great tumult in the cities, a fermata of sorts, or final stop to twenty years of expansion after the war, fleeting stretto, fleeing, the score coming to an end, endgame amid clamor.

The paradoxical sign of a subsiding élan, vaguely perceived as such despite the euphoria, a sudden start with no follow-up, something was dying, everyone felt it, which would never live again in the same way.

Much later on would spring up again perhaps, on a century scale, after the fin de siècle, and its drowsiness.

Slowly would be reborn from the torpor.

The place does more than anchor life, Martin didn't have many points of comparison until now, but he registered the phenomenon.

The place is endowed with a life of its own, he noted, it invests the body of the person inhabiting it, molding him to its space. Confers him with automatic reactions that are precise, exclusive, durable.

It's a self-contained universe. If I change places, I change worlds, he muses, and bodies as well.

Thus, after several months, his place of exile has become a world. His bents of habit have marked the way his body and his bearing hang together, his former bents smoothed out to the point of almost disappearing. He catches himself one evening reacting as if he had always lived here; disconcerted, must call upon his memories to drive off this idea.

What's in play is repetition, a slow immersion, the relegation to very limited trips, the impossibility of stepping back, of putting oneself at a distance, blocked in upon this territory and virtually immobilized, taking inventory of it by night most of the time.

Prohibited to overstep the city limits and its immediate out-skirts, without first obtaining a special pass, he found out the regulation is in effect for all this country's citizens as well, he converses with them rather often while moving about from one floor to the other, in brief snatches, with the men especially, with the women it's risky, all relations being forbidden, a high price to pay.

The home front as hardened as the front, finally, on alert, each civilian attached to his work station as if physically bound, machine or office, the police keep watch, people hardly chat, watch their words, or watch themselves between words, never speak without first glancing around.

"Be Silent, the Enemy Is Listening," is read everywhere on the city walls. And also: "Wheels Must Roll Quietly for Victory," as if they hadn't been already requisitioned so very many years ago.

One day Martin makes a thoughtless mistake, transposes two boxes, creating a certain disorientation in one of the workshops, thus a loss of production. Sabotage, it is declared, the police get involved, he is questioned, his case investigated.

The police chief surprises him, proves to be very nervous, raises his voice for no reason, seemingly ferocious, then grows calm all at once, despondent, muddled, almost imploring.

He doesn't report to the factory management, Martin suddenly understands, but to the secret police in the city. Is long past youth, must have gotten his hands slapped more than once. Martin explains himself, speaks a little German at present, slips out of this tight spot. But he's gotten noticed, his name noted in a file.

In his comings and goings from underground to rooftops, voluntarily passing on short messages and news, he's made two friends, Jitomir and Gunther.

Jitomir deported from Ukrainia, spokesman of his city by his family name, works on the second-level basement on an automatic tower, arms in oil all day long, an oily mist collecting on his hair, face, in his eyes, effusive with sweeping gestures and shouts, voluble, loves to joke around. He and Martin get along well, without understanding each other for all of that, wait for each other in front of the fence at night, keep each other mutual company from the factory to the camp.

Gunther, on the other hand, is reserved, a modest, unassuming demeanor. Very nearsighted, rejected by the military. Pale complexion, hollow cheeks, keen eyes behind steel-frame glasses. Operates an elevator in the warehouse, maintains the vehicles as well, sees to the fuel, deliveries.

Doesn't speak French, cuts short the conversations in the warehouse, canteen, but wishes to converse, wants to talk, it's clear. After a few weeks, invites Martin to his home.

One evening, a Saturday. Martin has the address in his head, is somewhat familiar with the neighborhood, has already passed by there several times. It's an itinerary he likes very much, along Insel Schütt—the large, then the small—the narrow wooden bridges on the Pegnitz, am Sand on the right bank, then one of the streets going up toward the Burg, Rotschmieds—or Thalgasse.

It's pitch-dark, rubble on the sidewalks and dirty snow on the rubble, eight o'clock, the shops have already closed, a few passersby bundled up, hands in the pockets of thick coats, plumed hats, fur-lined bonnets.

Shut-up dwellings, drawn curtains, where the cracked open windows, the panes shattered here and there, poorly plugged, allow through the sound, from a tavern with camouflaged facade whose door opens suddenly, giving way to the music, the astonished stroller can follow the radio-transmitted concert in perfect continuity right down the line, the one and only program, common to all, wedges block the dials on the sets in public places, and in private, the fear of being turned in for illicit listening is too great.

The piece being broadcast is one Martin knows well, by heart, Germanic to a fault, medieval, enchanting; a famous overture, the leitmotiv developing in the intricate division of the chords, expanding gradually, solemnly, as the improvised auditor with difficulty trudges forward through the narrow street, splattering in the mud, stumbling over the cobblestones.

The music arrives to perfect the scene exactly, it belongs to a whole, of the whole that is visible in these gables, flowered balconies and sloping roofs, in these cramped, twisted roads, in this particular path traveled through a prestigious city, possessing an aura of legend. Even the odor of the smoke in winter harmonizes with it.

It's too beautiful to be true, he thinks, recollecting this instant later on, I won't believe it. He knows that memory will betray him, delude him, mix up the scene. Knows that what in this place he sees, hears, will be poorly safeguarded, poorly restored, or barely credible with the passage of time. Or erased, plainly and simply.

He listens that much more keenly, all ears, to fix the place well, authenticate the setting. Steps along the middle of the walk-way, from two sides the sounds reach him in equal measure, the tempo has accelerated and the movement culminates in the tutti of the brass and the cymbal accompaniment, triad held a long moment in the fortissimo of the recording and its muffled echo at street level.

Decreed, obligatory unanimity, willful imposition of a sensi-bility, of a style of fervor, one that's national, this music would bear the brunt if it didn't lend itself so perfectly to this purpose by its own nature, but the others bear the brunt of it, he muses, and the narrow street opens out at its far end, emerges on to a wider road, Judengasse, that Martin is presently going up while the triumphal song fades very quickly, soon breaks through only in snatches behind the facades; he approaches flush alongside the windows, makes out the broken subsiding finale of the great symphonic exaltation, its jarring, dashed harmonies, its lost, disintegrated notes.

Unwarranted recapitulation of the cadences, paltry formulas, chromatic echolalia, more and more choppy, faraway.

On Egidienplatz, Martin doesn't hear anything anymore, there is no more harmony, no more support for this architectural array, silence, a bomb crater at his feet, black mud at the bottom, the church towers threatening collapse.

The weather's taking a turn for the worse, storm in sight, a heavy shower, it's about time.

Expectant, seated in front of the window on the garden chair, in front of the table, inert.

Coming back to my pet hobby, obsession. Stronger than me, begun again.

Surely not alone in being amazed, of course, in wondering what happened, things moved too quickly, we weren't on guard.

But alone here in any case, in questioning, in revisiting the times, places, in wondering why, how, monologuing, conjectures, refutations, impasse.

Impressed by this concern, a one-track mind, distracted from my work, nose in the air.

When I come up with nothing around four o'clock, noting down a word and crossing it out, searching for what doesn't quite fit and not finding it, finding that everything doesn't fit, that nothing works anymore in this business of voices and microphones, then I stand, push the table against the wall and put away my papers, simply dissatisfied nothing more, ever since the time this story came to a standstill.

Am going for a stroll up to the road, or around the pond where the pooled water has imperceptibly evaporated, potter about the kitchen, the living room—in the large house where there was so much to do years past, much more certainly than pottering about, that's why I left it, every morning spent dusting, washing, repairing, replastering, redecorating, repainting, I was working with music, the music station was still broadcasting, there was more and more interference, less and less audible, fell silent for good at the turn of the year.

The two local radios that I still picked up went off the air shortly afterward, there remains a commercial station with so-so reception, too much static, never any news, just ads, light music, hackneyed hits, series of trashy game shows, lugubrious ripostes, phony listeners' mail, they're playing the exact same tapes, I honestly believe, have programmed everything in a continuous loop and closed the doors, it's running all by itself, so feeble-minded what's the use, no need to listen anymore, to watch over the tapes, not even to erase them.

Will be erased all by themselves with the passage of time, will crumble, dust, all those inanities, bastard debates on all-purpose subjects, free-for-all roundtable discussions and phony conversations, skipped bits of info, sinister audios from broken-voiced idols.

Syrupy-voiced, doddering announcers, don't even give the

time anymore, and what's the point of commercials, nothing to
buy anymore.

I keep searching, you never know, searching on the dial, just to
be absolutely sure, longwave and shortwave and ultrahigh fre-
quency, pick up a voice sometimes on FM, 50 plus a little,
speaking Swedish, or Danish, uniform delivery, as if for itself,
what's it talking on about this way, without a break, at night also
perhaps, try tonight.

A magnetic phenomenon, some have asserted, on a grand scale,
lasting, in truth catastrophic. This crisis isn't only economic,
assured the mayor with a wink before disappearing last February.

What went off kilter, nobody knows exactly, it all fell apart
right down the line, then things accelerated lately, caught people
up short, on the wrong foot, irrevocably perhaps.

Divergent analyses in the beginning, vague, contradictory conclusions, a crisis in something or other, continental and who
knows what else, a crisis of confidence, or conscience.

Others spoke about flux and reflux, a classic theme, after a
boom, stagnation, expansion, recession, old familiar sinusoid,
that wasn't it either.

A new event evidently, occurring without any of the indexed
preliminary signs, puzzling, unpredicted, a wave too large to be
detected by the scientists, the specialists, the doctors. A mutation
of sorts, not only of the economy, but of knowledge, of memory,
within minds.

Sensed sometimes, in the prosperous years, and evoked in
veiled terms, brief symptoms, divulged, disowned, what of it
today, an alarm needed to be sounded, people stirred up, the
facts laid out in a public forum, the illness diagnosed, precautions
taken when there was still time.

Balance sheet of so many ages, disastrous, a century of bank-
ruptcies, everything was linked together obviously, monetary
disorders, televised gangrene, the leveling by the media, worth-
less ideology.

Five o'clock, here I am again searching, needle on the dial, sweeping the waveband, everyone in their own homes searching, simultaneously picking up this voice perhaps, everything that vibrates in the transitor, the only unanimity that's left, as long as the power stays on, naturally.

In Swedish, in Danish. What can this voice be telling itself, speaking for itself?

Tall narrow building, in one of the steepest of the small streets, not very far from Maxtor, opens through a side door upon a gloomy, vaulted vestibule, a blue-tinted lantern at the top.

Timeworn staircase, its worm-eaten railing, a lamp upstairs casts a feeble light on the eroded stone steps, hollowed out in the middle as if by a centuries-old trickle of water.

The draft makes the lamp sway, the shadows of the railing, the visitor danced on the walls, Gunther called from above, guiding the way up, and Martin reached the fourth landing, out of breath, surprised by the silence, not a sound behind the doors.

Gunther has use of one room and a kitchen that serves also as a toilet. A garret. He allows the view to be admired, extinguishing the lamp, parting the curtain, opens the narrow window and the cold is bracing, the old city can be seen, the Burg to the right, a glimmer on the snow here and there indicates a square, a street, a car bumping along.

The Burg is that dark mass looming against the sky vaguely brighter in the west; castle, Sinwellturm rampart walk, its roof with broken corners, imperial stables flanked by their two four- or five-sided towers, monumental background dominating the ordered lines of the tiered edifices on the southern slope of the hill, as far as Theresienstrasse and the river.

The landscape appears saturated with compactly overlapping elements composed of oblique surfaces slanting at very diverse angles, seemingly juxtaposed, or fitted together in every manner imaginable, a relief puzzle, life-size model where the rows, double at times, of long skylight windows piercing the roofs form so many observation posts, periscopic slits retaining the snow even after it's been dislodged along the steep surrounding incline and been swallowed up in the crevasses of the tiny streets.

It's the extreme variety of angles which intrigues Martin, the picture is made up entirely of conjunctions and intersecting angles, very sharp for the most part, creating an intense geometric activity; luminous bands illustrate certain figures, relegating the others into the shadows, and this organized chiaroscuro effect brings to mind the famous scenes where, in the movie houses of his childhood, swindler acrobats and mad scientists hunted each other mercilessly through the medieval maze of fantastically fabricated plots.

Captivated, almost incredulous. But searchlights in the distance sweep the sky, reconfirming the actuality of the war, and his host entreats him not to let the cold in any longer, the coal stove draws poorly, warming up the room is such a project.

Gunther reshuts the window, draws the curtain. Really such a great calm on the floor. Old people used to live in the building, retreated to the countryside after the last bombardments, still haven't been replaced, no one left but the infirm elderly woman on the ground floor.

He set up a table, put together the best dinner possible in view of the rationing, there's no black market here, he says. The bottle of white wine, one he's had stored away for a long while.

Is approaching his thirties but looks older, very skinny, a little stooped, coughs a lot. Speaks of his parents, his life before the war. Was a teacher back then. Seems torn between discretion and the need to confide. He's confident, yes, it's the habit of confiding that's been lost, perhaps, so many things have happened which broke habits.

Martin, for his part, does his best to tell about his life, mountain vacations, law studies that he'd just begun and which a little night outing gone wrong had unexpectedly interrupted.

They quickly get back to the factory, to its oppressive routine, an obstacle to be negotiated daily, without fail, flawlessly, without a hitch. Being careful above all, contriving for rest periods without getting caught. The factory, and sleep, exhaustion. The wine, fortunately, introduces a certain distance between speech and place of reference.

Teacher, and unionized, Gunther suddenly resumes, bringing two cups of ersatz coffee. He seems to have started up again to continue but falls silent, with his spoon stirs the saccharin powder at the bottom of the cup.

Drinks the scalding liquid in sips and Martin measures a lack, a waiting.

Gunther sets his cup down and says: "I spent one year in a concentration camp. I can't talk about it, only imagine."

And getting up, goes over to rekindle the stove, pours on a pail of coal nuts, straightens the pipe that has a tendency to smoke.

Then he takes out a pile of magazines from the bureau at the foot of his bed, puts them on the table, and passing them in review, offers each in turn to his guest, drawing his attention to an article, a title heading, a photograph.

The cover of an illustrated magazine with a wide circulation stuns Martin. Dating from the end of '36, it shows lines of inmates in striped garb, escorted by guards with weapons in their fists, and the framed title announces: "In this issue, the concentration camp of Dachau."

Another periodical, the same year, offers a report on the city's celebrated carnival. A long float drawn by two horses carries along a pack of parade participants decked out in caricatural masks, elongated noses, ears sticking out from their heads, rapacious leers; an inscription on the side of the vehicle specifies cheerfully, as if the workings of fate were finally fair, the immediate destination: "Onward to Dachau!" The crowd on the sidewalk points with their fingers, bursts out laughing.

Gallows, on other plates, on the same main street, from which mannequins are swinging, enemies of the people it's said, shame of the nation, polluters of the race, profaners of the empire; signs on their backs stigmatize their crimes.

And other publications, issues taken at random from the weekly racist informer sheet, a litany of slander, calls for murder and sacking, defenestration and lynching.

Gunther says nothing, or says only: "Look, here, take a good look."

A mixing of genres, hodgepodge and blurring: between two hateful pamphlets, a harmless article on Schubert and Schumann, a eulogy on faith, a playful exposé of the virtues of sports.

And this in addition, in June of '33, the solemn installation of the new archbishop, a large procession from Lorenzkirche to city hall: at the head proceeds the prelate, between the Ministers of Culture and of State, both in the party uniform, storm troopers acting as marshalls, the young are part of the celebration, in uniform also, sealing the alliance.

An instructive press review, Gunther hasn't finished but suddenly perceives that it's ten-thirty, Martin has barely enough time to get back to the camp, will be back, that's a promise, shakes his friend's hand, goes down into the darkness and plunges into the cold, stumbles on the sidewalks, turns too sharply right after Theresienplatz and winds up behind Frauenkirche, on Hans-Sach-Gasse.

Hans Sach, a national glory in his old house at the corner of the street, a prolific and popular poet, shoemaker by trade, Meistersinger on occasion, lyrical in his appearance in the opera celebrating the city.

Tradition of the written word, theater, great music, see how they're betrayed in their destiny; poets of the past, singers and musicians, mobilized by platoons, parading past, wretched creatures, wearing armbands.

Martin, alarmed, lingers, in a bad way, sets off running.

Pool water whipped as if by a machine gun, leaves and pebbles lashed, I see before hearing, hear before feeling and now I run, drops spraying on the dust of the lane, the thunder still far off, suddenly closed in.

Seated on the stone wall at the edge of the pond, I was watching the leaves, following the streambed up to the meadows glimpsed out there between the trunks of the small trees, the extraordinary variety of leaves, scalloped edges, density, the differences in dullness or shine, nuances of hues, of movement, diverse arrangements in the airy state of swing and vibration, imperceptible stirring in the torpor, revealed by an insect's modest intrusion.

I can remain hours on end, before the leaves, rocks, earth, flowers, observing the fantastic intensity of life at ground level, nose against the twigs, petals, veins and branches, roots, minuscule heaps of compact matter, so dried out lately, crumbly, and everything that finds a place to live there, burrows in, passes through, around, skitters and escapes, slithers and hops, flutters, crawls.

Everything that crosses, travels along, surmounts, cracks and pierces, imbibes and undermines, decomposes, moistens, bathes and penetrates, animates, fecundates and invades, absorbs, assimilates, lives as a parasite on matter, invisible at human eye-level, not smelled, not heard in its astounding whispering, rubbing, rustling, racket.

I didn't give it all that much attention in the past, forgotten it I suppose, didn't feel all that attached, that connected. A renewed feeling of presence in the aging, dependent body, proximity of the earth, the skin wrinkles, waves of stagnant water, leaves kneaded with mud, split crumbled stone, a heterogeneous mixture at a certain point, it's time to prick up one's ear and press it against the earth, to pick up the beating, the movement of the cycle and draw closer to it, to harmonize one's own cycle with it, to model one's own upon it.

What I perceived, my eyes following the shapes of the leaves, while going up the stream's course, sprays splashed up from the water, drops smacked the rock, I took to my heels, I ran toward the house, closed doors and windows, heavy downpour, the water from the heavens after so many days, holy water.

The thunder boomed all at once, very loudly, had fallen quiet when closing in, stored up, and now it's sounding the tonic "la," dramatizing the landscape, transcending the long mute stillness, the deferred period of waiting for rain, instantaneously torrential, with no prelude, interposing a moving veil between the panes and the flooded banks of the basin.

Pattering on the roof tiles, I check all the exits, cut off the power, unhook the antenna; thunder an echo of war, the nerves associated the sounds, ancient terror, this pause between flash and roar hangs heavily, a circuit imprinted, absolutely once and for all.

Expanding din, audible for ten leagues around, the isolated beings in what's left of the cottages take delight in unison at the propagating wave, a cosmic communion, each his own thought for the person hit by the bolt.

Rare unanimity nowadays, return to the sources.

In the past, a long-distance aircraft used to fly over at the stroke of noon, gave the time to thousands of fine folk, as it raced northward; a fighter sometimes broke the sound barrier, imitation hedgehopping, panicking the animals. Flying low overhead, an abolished custom, the sky isn't rent anymore except by lightning, the storm rumbles, its center a little to the west, the bulk over the Lot valley, a real river this evening, or a torrent.

I remain marveling at the strange transit of nebulous electricity in a state of potential collision and discharge. Beneficial drenching, all things come to an end.

Odors of the *causse* after rain, on the undergrowth, the moss. Taste them this evening. Or tomorrow.

The visit to the Burg, Martin has been postponing it for months, doesn't really know why. He'd go in winter, it'd be beautiful in the snow. Now winter's almost over and he still hasn't gone up there.

Has often passed at the foot of the rock, walking along the

retaining wall as far as Vestnertor, then the very wide ditch beyond the walls, going around the castle through the vaulted door in the ramparts and winding up at am Olberg, going down to one square or the other, Albrecht-Dürer, Adolf-Hitler, both on the river path.

He only likes fortresses when seen from afar, in the background of the stamp. The high enclosed edifice, its dark forbidding rock, the idea of crossbows and boiling pitch, immense flagstoned rooms where people die of exposure, besieged, starving, menaced by arrows and cannonballs from all sides, are all things that never attracted him, except when described in Gothic novels or inhabited by vampires.

At last, one Sunday in March, on a sudden impulse, he passes under the monumental portico, tells himself it's still time, mounts the ramp, goes all the way up to Sinwellturm whose wobbly pinnacle caps the wooden rampart walk, then retraces his steps, roams in the palace courtyard, briefly admires the wooden staircase, returns into Luginsland, leans his elbows on the parapet and contemplates the tiered planes of the roofs, the twin churches, the theater cupola emerging from the patches of smoke a little farther off, the suburbs to the south and the clear line of the forests over there in the sunlight.

Observed from here, the city appears rather untouched, the rubble at street level can't be seen, a few roofs are smashed in, beams charred, sections of wall knocked down, but the general look of the town is intact, the ancient organization of space safeguarded.

Leaning on his elbows, he has a sudden vision, a hallucination, the whole city destroyed, flattened, burnt down, and not a human being left, not a sound, nothing but the birds, he hears the birds, momentary fissure, a swaying, and everything is restored, alive.

This is indeed the city he heard about, medieval, mythical, inhabited by Meistersingers, hearty drinkers and toy soldiers; the one that picture books illustrated for him, popularized in his head, masterpiece of a nation whose name acted upon him to reveal prestigious deeds and legends, an initiator of culture, reserve of magic tales and Olympian hymns, age-old theater of fugues and counterpoints, a grand musical edifice.

The very name of the country seals this mythology of childhood, crowns it, adorns it with a disquieting, irrational charm, transmitted from generation to generation and reaching him without his ever asking why: the spell was something taken for granted.

A few Sunday strollers had the same idea as he and are sauntering between tower and palace, fountain and court, lean their elbows on the parapet, contemplate their city. The associations this name has for them he can't say, tries to associate it with the names of his country, space of awakening, of adolescence, but the names conflict at present, thwart each other, something snaps in the shock of terms.

A little later on, turning around, once again considering the decapitated tower, its blackish-brown stones with suggestions of glazed pink in patches, he understands all at once that he's living upon two territories here within the same time frame, continuously, upon two spaces within one, lodged in the same place, the same city, one within the other, and these spaces don't join, don't communicate, don't coincide at any point.

It's been that way since he's arrived, the territory bears the requisite name, is laid out accordingly, but what he has under his eyes tallies poorly with the period reproductions, the place corresponds without existing fully in the present moment, and this blinking back and forth between rival sensations, this gap, this twitching or minute beating is something he erases with words, without even being aware, neutralizes, annihilates by an instantaneous, conditioned, automatic reflex.

Represses at the very least one hundred fifty years of history in those moments, in that reflex, which protects him, blinds him also, but does he really want it, thrown into confusion by this perception of his condition, of his situation in this matter, of his position.

It's not his fault, he tells himself, things moved too quickly, caught him short, on the wrong foot, too many unexpected events came up these last years, astounding, insane, he wasn't able to focus, take a clear, exact view, nor assimilate them of course, they changed the world from top to bottom, turned it upside down, unrecognizable.

Surely not alone in wondering what happened, was too young, fourteen when the war broke out, and fifteen when the ground of his own country cracked, trembled, when his knowledge went to ruin, his ideas, his memory.

The ground of his childhood gave way under language, language still adorns the forms of the past, halos them, invests them, and the young man caught between the layers of this language is at wit's end as to what land he should dedicate himself, what words to be won over by, as to what grammar he should consecrate his body.

A feeling returns, a vague feeling, which grips him, often returned, unformulated, barely breaking through, and now it's suddenly expressed: a loss of identity in this upheaval, this debacle, the past names irretrievable, with no recourse, irrevocable, he feels he's an orphan, no country anymore, no family anymore, no school, no ties.

The wavering redoubled here under the cover of this land, in the deceptive mirage of this place, he leads a double life here, his body split by a line not traced under his steps, dividing his steps, his words, his thoughts, a border at every step, every glance, every sound.

Two halves in each day, every day, with no points of contact, except for a painstaking work on the why of causes and effects, the how of deeds unfolding, on the meaning of history, or its chaos.

From the massive tower with corners sheered off slantwise, decapitated, he turns away, and going back down along the steep ramp as far as the door under the surrounding wall, soon plunges again into the urban network of narrow streets.

Tells himself that the Empire-era stables still remain to be visited, flanked with their four- or five-sided towers, it's this Sunday or never, treats himself to the visit, as long as he's there.

Torture museum, full of invention, of verve in dislocating and mutilating and twisting, the Iron Maiden sublime in her corset of patched iron, dark carnivorous matron. He doesn't linger, leaves the place swiftly, lands his two feet back in the century, returned to his first condition.

Orphan, exile, and what else?

By making a fair copy of things, one loses one's qualities, characteristics, talismans of childhood.

Badly off, no doubt whatsoever, off to a bad start in life.

It rained the whole evening long. In buckets during the storm, a wind rose, driving off the cloudbursts; when it died down, the deluge turned imperceptibly into a shower, I installed myself on the doorstep, looked at the water falling on the oaks and junipers out there at the end of the meadow, the stones shading toward mauve and, closer by, the hyssops on the embankment on the other side of the dirt path, their long stems flung about, blue flowers dashed, which had already been withering.

Soft colors, transfigured by the smells, green and blue, purple, yellow, smells linked to the sound of drops striking and trickling, a steady beating on the packed soil under the drainspouts and the roof arris, fitful under the branches in the puddles that formed, overflowing onto the path ruts.

Sounds of striking in relief upon a background curtain, illusion of a continuous rustling in the atmosphere more luminous now in early afternoon, the large black clouds have dissipated with the thunder.

Smells, sounds and colors unified during the time of perception, in a state of dependence and resonance, and touch interferes, far off, prerecorded, an unctuous recalling of contacts, hand upon rock or leaf or damp wood.

The perceived object imposes itself through its difference, to the detriment of those absent which in turn enter the dance despite everything, their arrival disturbs the game according to rules that escape us, impromptu memory, association of ideas, an image sprung from a secret depth, ragbag of the past, storehouse of miracles.

I'm seated on my doorstep, the air grows cool without getting cold, watching the rain after so many days and listening to it, smelling it, when suddenly flashes along the road, in the hollow of the valley, a girl on a bike, pedaling at a good pace.

White jeans, pink pullover, floating hair, at the bottom of the slope, passes by, the sound can't be heard, takes advantage of the momentum.

I stand up, shout, the poplars conceal her on the hillock before the farm, she didn't turn around, did she hear, didn't turn her head toward the house, I run up to the road, no longer in sight, I call out.

Waited there the whole evening, never saw her again, didn't pass by again, it was in February or March, noted it on a piece of paper, never saw anyone on the road again since that day.

Pure chance, I was looking that way, on that morning, crossing the courtyard, and the incident took place, very simple, disconcerting, that girl pedaling, hair in the wind.

She hadn't crossed paths with anyone in the village apparently, I never knew, not only the surprise, after such a long while, on that deserted road, the astonishment in the present moment, but also a transferral, referral to another space, another world, one I had under my eyes however, I still do, it's the same setting, the same place, but the actors have disbanded, they made up the world two, three decades ago, played the scenes, improvised, they replay them only when sparked accidentally, bygone world passed into the shadows.

Unpaid actors, volunteers, only realized afterwards that they were playing, improvising, a distant era, we all got together in the summers, something was alive, followed its course, progressed, a general movement after the war, a general momentum and élan, we found it normal, natural.

We searched, invented, asked ourselves what we were doing, what it might resemble, had doubts, compared, started over, called ourselves into question.

You know only afterwards, understand only afterwards that you've been recorded, filmed, and that's where the trap lies, perhaps she knew it, the one smiling amidst us, rather taciturn, hair in the wind, would run through the meadow, laugh, turn around suddenly and stare at me curiously, knew that she was playing perhaps, that she was being trapped, it's so far off.

Twilight, a beautiful glow beyond the *causse*, fine drizzle, I'm comfortable, here, it's always the same setting, the same road at the end of the path.

The fact there's only one actor left is another story.

And the play's not at all the same.

Never-ending thaw, muddy sidewalks, the roadway turned into a stream, in the places where the spouts are broken, an oily, miry water stagnates, don't know where to step.

Martin tries to vary his itineraries, takes Jitomir off toward the fields of the Wöhrd and the shores of the river before returning to the camp, but Jitomir's only thought is to get back to his own people as quickly as possible, cook, sleep; any attempt to discuss the war in the east and the battle in his country comes to a sudden end.

Every evening it's the same picture in the academic edifice where the fine arts were taught in the past, where now all that's taught is respect for the eleven o'clock curfew and the strict blackout orders; Martin, the other night, exasperated by the bugs haunting his straw mattress, burned the thing in the courtyard and the watchman in black fell upon him, the blaze signaled the city from a distance.

Gave up trying to take along his compatriots, they feel

comfortable in there, having something to eat in the crowded, foul-smelling premises; a very recent arrival is part of the barracks, untalkative, scrawny, tattooist by trade, swore he'd tattoo the student; doesn't go out either, never seen eating, only drinking and smoking, pallid complexion, dark purplish skin.

So, alone, Martin leaves, strides at a good pace around the Ring, rounding the main post office, the train station, the theater, pushes on to Plärrer on the days his legs feel up to it, comes back by Jacobsplatz and Ludwigsstrasse. On other evenings, he has to force himself, reaches the center with difficulty, splattering through the melted snow, crosses Königsstrasse as if groping his way and rushes into the Mautkeller, locates a free seat in a corner from which he'll be able, while resting, to observe the diners calmly.

It's a vast basement restaurant, under the Mauthalle, late fifteenth-century Gothic, a very simple menu, soup, single entrée, dessert, priced within range of everyone's budget, the only guarantee these days of the term "socialist" joined to the regime.

This crude but substantial meal is something Martin can offer himself from time to time, a modest sum is allotted each week for canteen tickets and camp lodging, with some change left over for dinner and spare time activities.

He's therefore here in his corner, watches the people coming and going between the cellar's massive pillars, eating swiftly, silently, for the most part, the waitresses in black dresses bringing the dishes; sometimes exchanges a few words with a table companion who sees Martin reading the paper, but certainly not to comment on the news.

One evening, a man turning grey, in his sixties, who hadn't said two words from the beginning of the meal, orders a beer and, sipping it slowly, out of the blue speaks to Martin about the war, the one he fought in France, tells about the sieges, the trenches, to Martin's surprise expresses his utter contempt for the enemy's commander-in-chief who in '17, for example, had the mutinous troops decimated.

Says nothing about this same man becoming chief of state on the occasion of a disaster, but incriminates the Allies for their weakness in controlling and safeguarding the peace: it was necessary to react, in '34, in '36, doesn't specify to what, but the context is clear.

Guilty, he adds, and responsible too, every nation guilty, even complicitous, for having allowed things to go on, allowed rearmament. He falls silent a moment, then finishes his glass, and staring at the young man: "Europe has reached its end, sir, it's meted out its own death."

On this note, stands and bows his head, takes leave of his chance conversation partner, heads with slow, very straight steps toward the twin staircase at the back of the room and Martin can't get over it, doesn't believe his ears, it's the first time a German met at random has spoken to him so freely, so categorically, he thinks the man needed to say that at least one time, he had it on his mind and deemed it a good opportunity.

His words have their effect, Martin repeats them to himself, would like to remain a few moments more but the people standing are growing impatient and he must be off.

Climbs the stairs, nose down, then goes up Königsstrasse along the bumpy sidewalk between the puddles of intermixed snow and salt, passes under Frauentor, crosses the wooden bridge bordered by the branches of bushes growing just about everywhere in the ditch.

Walks across the Ring between two trams and winds up as if unawares at the central train station, mechanically enters the vast hall, sits on a bench in one of the rare free seats and studies the cupola that a shell seriously damaged during the last bombardment.

Twisted iron, lopsided masonry, on the point of crumbling it seems, surprising that people are still allowed to pass that way.

A vague commotion, sounds of footsteps more than conversations, a loudspeaker announcement raises heads, and Martin notices that he is sitting between two soldiers, both dozing, exhausted, beaten-up greatcoats, their bags jam-packed between their mud-splattered boots, looking like they've come out of a trench, he tells himself.

The man to his left cracks an eye open, asks the time, almost ten, says he's come from Italy, on his way to Russia, transit between two fronts, hasn't the strength to continue, closes his eye.

The whole hall is full of soldiers, the majority asleep, on benches, the floor, heads on their packs, three others in a corner chew pieces of black bread, pass around a flask, opposite the immense poster on the wall over there: "Victory, or Bolshevik Chaos," flaming letters, blackened by the recent fire.

At the entrance to the corridor leading to the tracks, the traffic board indicates the trains on the point of departure. One train is going off westward, in less than twenty minutes, express to Württemberg, then to Baden, then beyond the Rhine, the land lately annexed under the name "Westmark." Beyond that, the border.

One whole night, one whole day, two changes at least, no passport or travel permit, one whole night in the car with an eye open for the conductors, the express allows only a few chances, Martin tells himself, it's not the right way to do it.

To travel in stages, buy tickets for very short trips, that won't arouse attention, don't dawdle in stations, don't get noticed, this is really the first time he got the idea, what's making him dawdle here?

An order shouted from somewhere or other, and the soldiers get up, gather their bags, trudge off, slowly down the corridor toward the tracks.

Martin gets up in turn, watches them moving away, then leaves the station, turns onto Marienplatz after Bahnhofstrasse, with heavy steps reaches the camp.

Arranged in the cabinet serving as a library, the few books taken here, the small house a desert island, handpicked all in all, the others, the great number of others left back there, under lock and key.

A long while since I've reread any, Diderot two years ago, I was fixed on sensations, perceptions, traces in the body, to start everything over from the beginning, from one point, no, from nothing at first, then one living point, then just one being, because I am indeed one.

I am unable to doubt, he would say, that's precisely what I doubt, and not only since last year, but my difficulty perhaps comes from a misconception.

A misconception about place, time, about memory, contiguity, continuity, almost an act of faith, it's experience that settles things, and definitively decides, my senses have rendered me nothing but discontinuity.

To resume the conversation, once again reread it, I'm drawn toward this but the gesture isn't carried through, take out the book, open it, a lassitude interposes itself, summer fatigue, or trouble with resuming once more, the act of reading too long neglected.

Like growing vegetables, a must for some time now, I keep putting it off from month to month, yet it would be easy, a square patch in the orchard out there, carrots, potatoes, radishes, lettuce, rather than all the canned food one might want, what will I do when the time for bartering is past, no doubt that's just why I'm waiting before setting myself to the task.

A certain abandon. Never was able to set a program for myself and stick to it, it's contrary to day-by-day desires. Want to read, tonight, but not badly enough however, through the window the sound of drops still chinking, trickling leaves, beautiful scent of grass, of weeds, brambles, nettles, thistles, a particular taste, smoky, peppery.

If I did a little gardening, I'd be able to smoke my tobacco in the evening instead of just standing there, arms dangling, starting to make the gestures in spite of myself, packing the pipe, lighting it, still a perceptible, depressing frustration.

Power still on, eight days without a cutoff, at least if they cut it off I'd begin reading again, wouldn't surrender to complacency, surrendering in old age, an irritating thought.

The diabolical screen isn't what it used to be, out of eighteen channels only two are left, where have the others gone, the time of splendor is over and done with, discussion shows and Hollywood series, variety galas, live sports; no more televised news, no more music, no more movies.

Poor quality of the dial or technical difficulties at the relay station, I don't know, but lines run through the picture, often fuzzy, the colors faded, sickly; the Korean series begun last year is imperturbably following its course, not a single variation from one episode to the other, carnage, strangulation, copulation and shrieking, exasperating dubbing, they all talk out of their noses.

For whom, one wonders, there mustn't be many receivers in good condition left, and this Colombian rock 'n' roll, these fake Malaysian music videos, these ageless wordless cartoons jumping about like shadow theater against an ill-defined background of English countryside?

A face in close-up sometimes, one I think I recognize, doesn't seem to have aged, the very same one from the past perhaps, they're replaying the cassette, between two commercial sequences of an outdated, astonishing, obsolete luxury.

Refinement of another age and start of the foundering, a media brew on a colossal budget, all people talked about suddenly was communication, each person in his own home cut off from others while living the same stereotyped instant, the same marketing slogan, breathless, emptied.

Culture derived from high-class images, alibi of business, culture of the past naturally, that of the present never brought up, "creation" they used to say in my young days, a load of rubbish, they didn't even understand why.

I jump from one station to the other for almost an hour, you never know, one fine night a surprise, a real face, a genuine word, a real Japanese film, a really dramatic series, oil and sex, rotten schemes, fat checks, something imaginative at last, you can always cross your fingers!

Around ten o'clock real coolness, a rebirth, rises from the drenched ground, a calm night.

Slugs, snails, your time has come!

Jitomir tried in vain to rouse him on the way to the factory, hearty backslaps, Martin isn't perky, that's the least he might say, has been finding everything too much for some time now, trouble getting up in the morning, trouble reacting.

Opened himself up to Gunther about this train idea, Gunther put an end to it: crazy, he said, not the ghost of a chance, your reassignment isn't so clear, your papers would be taken away again, they'd see they were mistaken, everything's still in order here, under tight control, supervised, the place you'll be sent to, better not to even think about it.

Very depressed, therefore, the only positive point is that he's coping better than most, physically, several are sick in the camp, he pictured himself sickly, susceptible, notices that he's holding up, after all, clings to this idea.

The others often ask him for advice, you're the student, for a paper, a translation, serves as interpreter on occasions, dictates a letter to the family, a nicely phrased message of love to a spouse, a fiancée.

Wrote home himself for the New Year, answer arrived in March, so manhandled by the censors that not much was left to read, everything was going well it seemed, subject to the blacked-out lines.

A rather tall brunette, pert-looking, in her thirties, just to the right on entering workshop 26, makes sheep eyes at him every time he passes, straightforwardly invites him back to her place, but he doesn't dare, it's too risky, everybody will be in the know soon, denunciation, gossip, plus she's too tall, he decides.

Evenings, he stays in the camp sometimes, breaking his principle, goes to have a beer in the café opposite, recrosses the street, reclimbs the large stone staircase with the enormous plaster heads standing starkly in the corners, tries to read in bed but it's not easy, the heat, the noise, and the cheap novels lent him are rather destitute.

The big event, in April, is the concert. Martin had already noted these performances, two or three times this winter, in a small hall near the river, had been on the point of going, hadn't let himself be tempted in the end, fatigue or inertia, the cold perhaps.

That evening, three quartets, Haydn, Mozart, Beethoven. The hall is a very old church, Katharinenkirche, adjoining the cloister, a shrine of the Meistersingers in the past, setting of the first act of the famous opera.

The hall is almost full, meditative atmosphere, the four instrumentalists are old musicians, with academic deportment, very nineteenth century, their phrasing a bit lyrical, romantic, beautiful ensemble tones, but what fascinates Martin is the banderole covering the entire pediment above the platform.

Red Gothic letters name the cultural league of the party, Strength through Joy, its initials located a little lower on the ring circling the cross, swastika from time immemorial, Aryan symbol of "good omen," sign of greeting.

Hung in such a way the swastika seems suspended from the precise base of the empty space between the players' music stands, talisman or sword depending on tastes, favoring the performances or hampering them, burdening them, according to viewpoint.

Dominating them in any case, conditioning them, sounding the "A" of an appropriation that is equivalent to diverting the meaning and function of the music, pending further information, the young foreign listener muses, whom this presence surprises —he ought to have been expecting it, however—and disturbs, not only due to a fundamental question but because, garish, crude and obtrusive as it is, he is reminded of the inscriptions or unpretentious banners decking the halls of open-air cafés and villages for local dances and club meetings. And the gentlemen in suits, down below, seem totally out of place.

The word "culture" diverted, the imposition of the swastika, and the very use of the word "strength" tacked to the first, these manifest three types of lexical perversion which had struck him only episodically until now, in the word "socialist" for example, or the expression "free worker" on his canteen card.

Usurpation, forgery, travesty of terms, tawdry trappings, debauched, depraved, a warping of language and everything it names, suggests, evokes, reveals, corruption of the field by contamination, derangement of the entire interplaying network, of the unconscious, of memory.

Haydn falsified, "sigh of Mannheim" heaved off the beat, as if regretfully, recycled, vitiated by the propaganda squad; Mozart tainted, the emblem's hooks quashing the quavers of the minuet, disguising the élan, the verve; Beethoven scoffed in his hymn, joy corroded by a strength held in contempt.

Martin has much trouble fixing his ears in the furrow of the chords; the pure moments of these musical pieces, as pure as any in existence, are stolen by the letters up above, confiscated, plundered, the swastika whirls and its hooks clip, shred.

Applause of the music lovers, for the instrumentalists, for the artists no doubt, rather than for the swastika, and now a lecturer comes forward on the stage, an orator, a messenger of meaning at any rate, who sets to vaunting "our" music and praising its virtues, its spirit, its purity, thus its supremacy, before launching into an exacerbated diatribe against all those other sorts which, degenerate, sully our century with their unwholesome inventions, suspension of tonality, polyrhythms foreign to our race, the cacophony of Negroes called "jazz," and the words come back in his mouth, each time more intense, the word "jazz," the word "Negro," as if the hysteria he ascribed to them was gradually possessing his voice.

Applause, the man withdraws, Martin is about to get up when the four old gentlemen, imperturbable at their posts, start into the slow movement of Haydn's quartet which has been the German anthem for a long while.

This is no time to move, you could hear a fly buzzing, the swastika presides over the ruse, its shadow reaches the stalls, conquers the entire space, a very dignified silence at the end of the piece, each person heads without breathing a word toward the exit, with muffled steps, it was so very beautiful.

Mild, clear night, it's springtime, Martin takes a few steps along the river, the word "jazz" mocked in its altered Germanic pronunciation remains stuck in his throat.

A famous melody comes back to him, Ellingtonian, very chromatic, refrain from another world, voluptuous, dreamlike, keeps him company on the way back.

Whether it's art or not, he doesn't at all know, and what do they know if the shadow of the swastika has the force of law?

The sensation of a repetition, revival of some stage business, somebody has most likely lived this, very far from here perhaps, I moving in his tracks, or perhaps they belong to a hero from a book, a haggard character leaving his buried den, entering a ravaged, deserted world.

Affront to history, after so much progress, so many discoveries and conquests, advances in science and knowledge. It was necessary to observe more closely, to discern the signs they'd been altering for twenty years, people didn't know how to read them in time, signs in the voices, in the music come from elsewhere, ambivalent, deceptive.

From another continent but they touched our own, called out to our own, interpellated it, designated it through its difference, drew an intaglio at this stage of history and it was necessary to listen to it more closely, Tina, to watch her point her arm, her finger toward the captivated audience, signifying its fate perhaps, a cocky humor in her voice and her cries, claws bared.

I put the cassette back on, Tina "live" in an old concert in a large European city, lewdly unbridled, hypnotizing those who thirty years earlier marched at this same age and held their arms out straight, which now they raise in benevolent rallying signs, signs of greeting, ecstasy.

Armbands before the war, and today bare-armed, bare-breasted girls rocking to the tempo dictated by the black woman swaying her hips, precise in her separate steps avoiding the onstage traps, microphone cords and skirting the footlights that change at each beat, each measure.

Short pink pleated dress upon strong slender thighs, suspenders baring her upper breasts, naked back, high black belt and black boots, golden earrings under her wild bushy blond mane.

Jutting cheekbones, hook nose, slightly swollen face trickling with sweat, straight narrow crack of the eyes set off against the very large oval of the mouth.

Radiant, fleshy lips sensually delighting in the high notes when the forehead almost touches suffering, contorted, furrowed, given over to love in its childish playfulness, mischievous, controlled frenzies, raptures, impish.

Symbolic figurine glimpsed from the last rows wriggling about, stamps in place, artificially stiff, mimicking the duck walk, jerky, body bent in two, falling, throwing itself back, imitating the act and the spasm, coitus with the microphones, knees bent, microphone in the mouth upon round lips beading with moisture.

Inordinately provocative in her renewed outburst, exasperated, fevered, designating the refused delirium, haranguing the one absent from the stage in the being infinitely multiplied in the darkness before her and whom she doesn't see raising its arms.

The preacher's strains in his overseas parish as he projects the pitch note of the spiritual into the body of his worshipers, tears of prayer on his transfigured face, voice striving for paroxysm in the hoarse high notes sliding into sublime lows.

Furious determination to seduce, conquer, as if it wasn't already accomplished with the very first steps, but the calling arms summon, stimulate, lure, seek the wholly devoted communion of bodies, but "soul" belongs to her alone, to her skin alone.

A crescendo varying with each number, very brief changes of expression, extreme mobility of facial features, vitality of each beat and offbeat, what majesty, languor, this is paradise she says, love's got no business anyplace else, what business has it got anywhere but here?

Tonality of the blues in Franconias, French and German communities, after slipping off returns in a white sweater and jeans articulating the buttocks, waist and breasts of a still very young girl, designates what is wholly desired, a word to the wise.

Signs spread thick, wholly passionate, sensual enjoyment rather than joy, and strength to boot, it's there, legible, that strength to perpetuate, renew, be reborn.

Strength to die and to be reborn, that's just what it is.

The lull is over, what was able to pass for a truce, and its minor violations, the air-raid warnings have resumed, harassments rather than regulation attacks, one or two in the night, almost every night.

A few rockets on a certain point, lighting the scene, plane fuselages caught by the projectors' beams, rapid-fire response, hail of bullets, explosions of isolated bombs, skirmishes, except for those who are below and helpless, but the objectives don't seem especially military, unless everything's strategic, military, the war will be total, declared the minister.

The noose is tightening, people feel it clearly, the uninterrupted retreat for months on end in the east feeds their fear, but there'll be a resumption of the offensive come good weather, it's a certainty, an invasion is needed for their faith to waver.

The newspapers say "invasion," they reassure, one's expected, all stand ready to repel it, contain it, they've been asserting this for months, talk of brand-new secret weapons that are going to change all the givens, turn the tables, the enemy will be caught short, duped, brought down.

Must hold out till then, consolidate the stronghold, shore it up, reinforce it with ditches, the fortress of Germany will harden its will by getting back to the basics, a great project is going to see the light of day, a grandiose film on the besieged city, Kolberg, its citizens risen en masse, mobilized, invincible.

Martin reads the news in the daily evening paper, entertainment column, they'd been talking about it for a long time, it's going to happen at last but time is of the essence, no point in building sets before long, he muses, things are evolving very quickly at present.

The great change for him came on the day when he learned that, starting immediately, he'd be on nightshift. He wasn't expecting this. Now here's a new twist to his dreary destiny of apprentice worker. It turns everything upside down, overnight.

Early in the morning, instead of waking up and leaving for the factory, it's to the camp he returns, to go to bed, sleep, dawn is breaking, he doesn't understand anything anymore, the pallid light attacks him, he fought sleep the whole night, nauseous, drowsy, an interminable night in the deserted workshop.

Only one machine is running, his own, only a few posts are occupied at night, and the big lathes in the basements. Only one lamp therefore, a narrow circle of brightness at one of the far ends of the vast premises, opposite the elevator door, and eyes against the lamp riveted upon the machine body quivering, vibrating, semi-automatic, that needs to be fed, watched over, lubricated with this sticky, foamy, runny liquid which often squirts in his face.

Watch over the smooth functioning, the production of identical parts, sorts of metallic primers or caps, firing-pin parts perhaps, feed the machine with aluminum cylinders, stop the electric motor at regular intervals to clean out the shavings.

A moment to catch one's breath and straighten up, turn around upon this darkness stretching as far as the eye can see, persuaded at that instant they've been forgotten here, or locked up, every exit blocked, that they'll never leave the place, a stage sunk in shadows, permeated with greyness, stifling, a dreamlike sluggishness.

Torpor, isolation, mental blackouts, swift dizzy spells, impossible to predict, head and chest bending, sinking, hands instantly groping for support, slipping, one hand always holding on to something.

The first nights are hard, he doesn't manage to get used to it, takes up his job come evening when the others are arriving back in camp, crosses paths with them in the street, until midnight holds up, until the break when a quick bite and coffee reinvigorate him.

After two o'clock comes the collapse, legs bend, hands stray, grope, eyes close, he doesn't know what he's doing anymore, how far he's gotten, for how long, repeated bursts of attention; he keeps the two organisms alert, his own not as well broken in as the other before him, the one clicking along, humming, industrious, assiduous, tireless.

At incalculable intervals, the elevator's iron door slides, all he sees is the sliding, and the man in black appears on the threshold, right before him, black cap, flashlight in hand.

A slightly stooped old man, double chin, protuberant nose, surely less tired because strolling about and sitting from time to time, who greets him, grumbles two words, withdraws into the light following the brief beam of his handlamp, the holster of the big revolver beating against his thigh.

At six o'clock, time off, a rest period from which he draws little delight, little profit, sleeping on the bedstead's straw mattress in the broad daylight; street noises, the sound the lame men make when entering, leaving, shouting, the sense of discontinuity starts all over again, the spasms, the nausea, the reverse side of a reverse side, nightclothes turned inside out.

Thrown off center, Martin, as if propelled toward the edges, and propelled again, repelled, his sense of balance is targeted, even when asleep, harassed when eating, jostled when dreaming, red eyes, losing his footing, down at the heels, yes.

Eats little, eats poorly, no more appetite, drinks poorly and much too little, grows thin, sheds flesh as people say, gradually falls into the mold of this diet, lives in a state of sleepiness, mental prostration, gloomy painful hallucination, rests a little better during the days in the long run but doesn't really fall into the rhythm, feels perpetually feverish, experiences a vague rush of excitement when passing through the gates at dawn, seeing the glow over the forest behind the train tracks, he thinks it's a memory.

Doesn't derive any benefit from the big weekend rest. Would like to take long walks on Saturday night, he's wide awake, but the fatal hour for returning to the camp cuts short his élan and in the end he hardly goes into the city anymore, dawdles on the Wöhrd between the branches of the river, sits on a bench, the grass and the new leaves on trees, soft on the eyes, soothe him, flowers about to blossom, he'd stay there until daylight.

Cycle completed on Sunday evening and the night repossesses him, tries to take stock but doesn't succeed, often wishes an air-raid siren would sound, he'd go to the shelter, be sitting down, he often cursed his cart, hardly remembers today what it was like, pushing along the vehicle and stopping in every spot for a chat, finding the time long.

A whole month goes by this way, but the events of his life no longer go hand in hand with those outside, he can't say where their history is inscribed, in what register, under what column, the very dates look scratched out, erased, rewritten.

One week later, surprise, Gunther is in the canteen, nightshift too, in the warehouses, at a moment's notice replaces an injured employee, he can sit down, doze, go off for a bit.

It's a godsend, a comfort, in the depth of the night Gunther with his drawn features, circular glasses, emerges from the zone of darkness, comes up to Martin, a piece of cake, a beer, coffee in hand.

Lingers whenever he can, seems to bear the change of status better than his friend, comments on the news, on the lookout for the slightest clue in the communiqués, the slightest sentence, and a reason for hope.

One evening, midnight approaching, the iron door slides, Martin, nose to his machine, watches it slide, spots Gunther on the threshold of the workshop, opposite him, up close, paler than ever, serious, almost solemn, who drops these words, a glimmer in his eyes, voice steady without being raised: "Martin, the invasion's here!"

A walk through the *causse* after the rainfall, clear sky in early morning, clayey puddles in the ruts of the path between the meadows, covered by thistles, the barbed wire of pastures buried under the networks of brambles, broken branches, stones split off from rocks a little higher up, the place where begins the forest of oaks and junipers, maples too, and the undergrowth of mother-of-thyme, thyme, marjoram and all sorts of grasses whose names I often asked about and were often told me, to no purpose, only a few names can be retained from the vast lexicon.

I turned left at the first crossing, this trail rather wide in the past, branches stretch across it today, just enough room to pass, this is the spot where a snake under an oak had raised its head one day and hissed in our direction.

It was within reach of the pitchfork, seemed ready to dart forward and we stood motionless several minutes, then it wound around the very thick trunk, climbed, fell still halfway up, measuring a good six feet and we stepped back, dumbstruck, not daring to pass, it could still dart forward.

Smells of leaves and moist barks, it was a beautiful shower, bright sunshine at present, loose soil under foot, low drystone walls and, here and there, heaps of crumbled *caselles*, there's a dolmen in a certain place, I failed to find it these past years, I'm mixing up two sites perhaps, try to get your bearings in this undergrowth.

As for the paths, I find them again easily, the sharp-angled one at the second crossing leads within sight of the abandoned farmhouse at the edge of the cliff overlooking the narrow valley to the west, abandoned before the incidents, for a long while, cattle used to camp all around, would advance upon you as you approached, slowly, solemnly, as if to dissuade you from overstepping the boundaries.

Used to come by bike also, cutting a path to this lost place where several *caselles* in ruins formed a hamlet in ancient days, but what days they were, coming back by this straight road, stone-paved in places, a coach route some said, as far as the iron-cross intersection near the dilapidated cottage where a lone fellow erected a farmyard, saw to a vegetable garden, all alone with his dog in the middle of the *causse*, his dog, his cats, curious there are no cats to be seen anywhere these days.

He's not there anymore, in any case, no more chickens, nor dog nor cats, nor anyone, the shack is disappearing beneath the dead branches and the nettles, the water tank burst, the cross itself sits askew, rusted upon the low limestone wall.

Isolated there, years on end, used to come and see him, a curiosity all in all, his red beard, the old rifle at the foot of his bed, now the curiosity would be myself, but no longer anyone to come suddenly upon me.

After the cross, there is a sort of meadow and it's a little farther on that I go wrong, every single time, not the first but the second footpath, the way straight to the village, I return home, along this vanishing footpath, guessing roughly through the thickets, cut across the trench, bare in the past, under the high-tension wire, get back to the path toward the small and large houses, both called farmhouses on the maps, I see them from a distance, the long blue-tinted slate roof of the large one, the tile roof of the small one, typical of the region, upturned at the bottom, Asian-style, the sloped corner on the sides evoking a sort of festooned cap at the very top of the wall.

Between the two, the pond, but I can't make it out from here, the foliage conceals it, that of the walnuts, of the ashes bordering the fields, the large linden's between the two houses.

It's my domain. A hermitage of sorts. Constant problem imagining the active life of years long past. The feeling sometimes that it lives on, elsewhere, on another star, my body has its part to play, as do all bodies, woven with letters, ciphers, figures.

All the past locations in a concentrated space, unaltered, representing their scene, mute utopia, my fantasy speaks volumes.

Then, this very one will be replayed there one day, the scene of the hermit leaving the *causse*, getting back to his house.

Summer. The smell of the leaves from the river along the factory path, he holds on to it a moment, precious asset for the night, one that the soapy water, grease, overheated metal have quickly driven off, all that remains is the idea of a summer night, the shadowy workshop expels it, it slips away.

At times he leaves the camp a little earlier, walks along the banks under the pines to the first bridge, the scent of pine follows him, resin, bark, needles; he'd entered the forest shortly after his arrival, a Sunday in summer, and the smell struck him, the fine layer of sand and the ferns, and the silence, the particular grey of the light.

Central Europe, he'd told himself, railway sleepers on the sand in the wide cutting between the rows of pines, straight tracks in the forest, and still this silence, had no inkling of it in his home region bordering the sea, another world, but the tales told of it, the ones he read as a child.

An air-raid warning in mid-June. He is sent onto the roof to put out the incendiary tracers lodged sideways in the tiles or cement by shoveling sand; he must stay there, exposed, vulnerable, with access to the shelter only if bombs explode.

So found himself up there, under the stars, planes flying over the city, with a German whose youth was long past, wearing blue fireman's helmets, both quite ready, at the slightest detonation, to dash down the stairs.

Thinking they heard one at a certain point, through the clear night, without a second's hesitation bolted, dove into an individual concrete shelter down on the sidewalk, huddled there, suffocating, until the all clear sounded.

Nothing was said to them, all the others already in the shelters no doubt, no one on the upper floors to register their flight.

Gunther, after two weeks, rejoins his day shift and Martin no longer has the comfort of his visits, remains alone the whole night long under the lamp and doesn't really grow accustomed, recuperates poorly, weakens.

One time awakens with a start under his machine, lying on the cement, nudged by the foot of the man in black. Had fallen asleep there, fainted, and the machine was running by itself. The man raised his voice, for form's sake, didn't pronounce the fatal word, drew away grumbling in the beacon of his flashlight. Martin is grateful to him, a quirk of this sort can cost him dearly.

Is demoralized, the night is never-ending, this trail is never-ending, will only end with the war, and that's not even certain, in one case at least. But the invasion has succeeded, the war will be over before winter.

Violent bombardment some while afterward, the Ring is gutted, the theater once again hit, a place he still hasn't gone; this is the opportunity no doubt, he seizes it, shaking off his torpor, gets a ticket for the following Saturday.

The performance is at seven, and it's raining that evening. By the large staircase he reaches the balcony. The damaged auditorium is a theater set in its own right. A bomb went through the roof, exploded in the orchestra seats, the slapdash repairs allow rain to drop on their makeshift seats in the spot where the hole was covered over, the members of the audience protect themselves as best they can, anonymous under their umbrellas.

Deficient lighting, the chandeliers have sunk, but stage and orchestra pit seem intact and when the curtain rises, suddenly set off against the ruined, dilapidated, dismal auditorium, is the sumptuous shimmering space of settings and costumes, both flawless, superbly lit.

Pompous, aggressive music, subtle in its excesses, Richard Strauss, his *Ariadne on Naxos.* Sensitive to the writing's baroque redundancies and witticisms, expressed in its spectacular oppositions and incessant distant modulations, Martin has much trouble following the unfolding action: words escaping him even more than on similar occasions in his native tongue, mythological deeds getting confused in his mind, he has eyes and ears only for the glittering effects.

And the staggering contrast between auditorium and stage. For in front of him out there, beyond the sphere of dismantled darkness, open to every wind, where the stoic faithful commune without flinching, it's a forgotten world that bares itself to the gaze, antique duplication, cultural splendor and pageant of the myth, its own myth as well, a historical fragment of the continent, of this twentieth century on the threshold of peace and very brief blossoming, that promised so much.

Two designs strangely intermingle here, two topographies one might say, the labyrinth's with its foiled circumvolutions, the score's whose delirious chromaticism tightly weaves the web in which opera hero and music lovers get caught.

A definite hysteria reigns on stage, masked extras, implacably logical in drawing out the rounds of the maze and in consequence altering the values of notes, the relationships of tones, the subdivisions and syncopations of tempos. The exacerbation extends to every point of the network, writhing bodies, entreaties, vengeful diatribes, thanksgivings to the gods and gesticulations, curses, an exacerbated tragification of every least sign.

A catastrophic horizon limits this universe, exclusively composed of song and dance but the menace pierces through with a sudden shattering burst of a collapse that will aim to be grandiose but won't be, a wished-for apocalypse perhaps, made plain and simply inescapable, by using such means, by courting such forces, by unleashing such tempests.

This whole jumble however—it can be heard in several dubious calm spells—remains marked by a touch of good form, if not good taste, a family affair, the bourgeois splendors of the adolescent century are played to the hilt, a bizarre impression, the castle of cards has already collapsed, quite some time ago, an opera ghost is moving about on stage, reanimated for the evening, in color, speaking, bellowing, singing, total cinema.

A contortion also, absence is party to this spectral revitalization of the work, as lyrical as one might wish, the absence of those its very presence ousts, expels, denies or excommunicates; they are there this evening, bearing witness on the sly to their lives in lands of exile.

It's well and good nevertheless, Martin tells himself, to put on theater at any price, in such circumstances as these, the war is raging, the fatherland is menaced, there are other fish to fry, but the theater is open, repaired any which way, the engagement honored at the appointed time, the entire cast present, as if everything were normal.

High-quality performances for a provincial city, but it's part of tradition in this country, it was often repeated to him, the states of the past have retained their courts, those of artists and doctors, singers, musicians.

After an hour's time, the uninterrupted reverberation of the melodic lines and their symphonic support have exhausted his faculties of attention. He found the word: respect. Respect for art, the things of art, the cult of art—of the past, preferentially, no boldness shown.

Not too much respect, all the same, he concludes. He's young, not much experience, not very cultivated yet, can be mistaken, but: not excessive, he repeats to himself, while big drops begin falling on the balcony rows.

On stage, a sun ever Aegean, if not Olympian.

It's the last performance perhaps, the bursts of Strauss in his tyrannical effusions are going to destabilize the vault, it will crumble at the cadence ending the act.

Martin gets hit on the head by a trickle, beats a hasty retreat, stepping stealthily.

To the right of the dirt path, even before cutting across the road, the small house appears in profile, built on the incline between pond and fallow fields, the long ground-level garage, living quarters above, reached upstream by the terrace situated even with the water tank.

The high wooden door of the garage follows the arch of the vault, in singular contrast with the festooned triangle of the cut corner of tiles at the top of the wall, slightly overlooking a small window in the stone where a statuette once stood watch in the past, empty today, leaving behind a suggestion of an amphora's imprint.

Panic upon returning, every time, but I wasn't thinking about it during the walk, carefree attitude, curious, happy all in all: and if somebody while I was gone had broken into my hiding place?

The last yards hurrying along, eyes on the door whose brown varnish has chipped, cracked; upon the lock, intact.

For more peace of mind, I make the key turn, crack open the door, and walking around the old Ford—looking pretty good considering it's twenty years old, raised up this way, out of fashion certainly but no more than the others, are cars still being manufactured?—go straight to the hole concealed by the woodpile, raise the cover of the tin trunk, yes, everything's there, tobacco and cigarettes, port, whiskey, pastis, and chocolate for myself, Christmas and my birthday, and the blessed day when I finish my play.

Household soap too, detergent, matches and candles. Near the entrance, the single carboy of gas, the last one.

Shut the door again, climb the hillock, walk around the water tank, when it goes dry the pond water will be left, don't worry much about it for all of that, there are more pressing matters, the question of vegetables for example, the problem of the vegetable garden still remains unsolved.

Soon it will be noon, ideal climate today, the grass still damp, gentle coolness, settle down comfortably in the kitchen, with sardines and beans, dry fruits, jam, a cup of coffee to wake myself up.

Rustle of leaves in the slight breeze, this side of silence, the great silence of the birds in August, mute invisible birds, save for the discreet blackbirds at day's end; the jays have broken off their noisy battles, crows, titmice, thrushes flown off, they'll be back in September, later on the falcons, vanished in the countryside.

And yet something's out there, brief cries, monotonous, one single chord, the accentor's no doubt, a kind of sparrow also called a hedge sparrow, male sparrowhawk or kestrel, tercelet, or barred warbler, or rail, bush warbler, I'm not certain anymore, I'd read that in the thick book left behind over there with the others, in the study between the billiard room and the main living room.

I go over once a month, into the large house. On the average. By way of a calendar I pinned a sheet of paper above the pantry, I mark the days down as they pass but have already made mistakes several times already, let some slip by, or counted twice, I take stock over at old Lambert's, he happens to make mistakes too, the post office woman has the final word in cases of conflict.

Will go tomorrow perhaps, or this afternoon, the time come around again, according to my records. Habituation, we all conform to this new life, a quickly acquired bent of routine. Still, it's not so old as that, this state of things, a decade at the most, everything fell into dilapidation much faster than was first thought, decomposed, more and more stupid on a mass scale, the social tissue come undone as they used to say.

Who might have imagined it? Transportation paralyzed,

machines out of service, circuits broken down, communications cut, it was unexpected, staggering. More serious is this resignation, this latent acceptance, as if unconscious, the absence of reactions, a sleepwalking tetanized populace, an extraordinary situation after what we'd experienced, very quickly turned banal, not one person lifted a finger, here at least, if that'd been the case elsewhere, we'd have found out about it, in the end.

I'm guilty as well, in a way, nothing attempted since last autumn, the last try, botched. Left alone on my bike along the Cahors road, bag on my back, determined to know, to be clear in my own mind, and see what condition the cities were in.

Inert sleepy cities, people watched me pass by, with no surprise, no curiosity, no expectation. After eighteen miles I got a flat on the gravel, several times in a row, nothing left for repairs, no one to help me, direct me, comfort me.

Returned, stopping frequently, pushing my bicycle, dead tired, very gloomy. Haven't moved since.

To leave again on foot, aimlessly, yet another try to get myself out of here? Or wait for what, for this to pass, for the wind to turn, for something in sight perhaps?

Wait for a sign, like before, the least sign, a blinking?

The century is drawing to a close, a millennium, the end very near. To leave again—on another foot.

It would be high time.

The night has come to an end, so he's notified by late September, and Martin with no regret, with no further ado, swaps it for the day, overnight. He reconverts himself, after four months of enforced isolation in which he did everything backwards, if not against the grain, again finds himself among his "family," if such a word may be used, in the factory as well as in the camp.

Works with the others, moves from place to place with them and not in the opposite direction, eats with them, sleeps with them. Sees Gunther and Jitomir again. Nothing's changed, except that the cook, due to trafficking in foodstuffs, was arrested and never seen again.

Martin was promoted to milling-machine operator. Standing before his mill, he sharpens drills throughout the day, minimal cone-shaped metal surfaces with curving diabolical edges, the lamp's reflections often blur the cutting edge, a great precision required, no trembling, he takes some time in adapting, in getting the knack, in bringing his arms, his fingers under control.

Russians around him, one Pole, the German foreman, a Frenchman in his forties, grinding-machine operator by trade, ill-tempered, finicky, talks only shop.

It's on one fine October morning that someone comes for him there, the police chief is waiting, and with an exasperated air dryly hands him a summons to appear immediately, the matter is urgent.

Police station, Department of Aliens. Martin is surprised. The good fellow raises his arms to the sky, assures him that it's beyond him, then, gentler, pushes him toward the door, cordial, almost consoling.

Disconcerted, Martin walks the whole way, crosses the city for the first time on a weekday morning, goes along Lorenzkirche, Karolinenstrasse, is impressed while entering the immense building where uniformed orderlies, deciphering his paper, on each floor dictate to him the correct procedure.

He waits on a bench, the Department of Aliens indeed, it's written on a door, the door opens after a long while and he is made to enter.

A seat across from a state worker in civilian clothes, rather tall, in his thirties, attentive gaze, inexpressive, who takes a file from a stack, consults a few papers, goes to get the interpreter.

The female interpreter is twenty years old, pretty, ash blond, a light-cloth low-cut dress, comes in flitting about and says: "Hello, I speak seven languages, everybody calls me Snow White here." And she sits down, crosses her legs, smiles.

Seems to be at ease in these offices, does as she pleases, and

Martin, staggered, intimidated before he even entered, hasn't any idea how he should act.

The woman translates what the other reads, without looking at him, smooths her hair, adjusts her dress over her thighs, explains to the foreigner, in a nonchalant, carefree, weary voice, that he is accused of having made seditious, subversive and dangerous statements in the workshop.

Martin opens his eyes wide, understands fairly well what the man is saying, which gives him a little time to sort things out, listens very surprised, very bothered, what has been reported he's said in the workshop?

Said one day, quite plainly, to someone intrigued by the fact that there were so many foreign "volunteers" in the factory, that as for him and his workmates, certainly not, they hadn't come voluntarily.

Said another day that there were, in his country, a number of men evading conscripted labor and that it was easy, in the countryside, to shirk the laws, and hide out.

These evaders gather in groups, make up networks, have links abroad with terrorists, saboteurs, in Italy especially, in Serbia, Croatia.

Assured on a certain day that such groups existed here too, highly organized, highly trained, ready to act.

Germany in these conditions has few chances of winning the war, the die is cast, it's only a matter of weeks, days maybe.

And it's not over, Snow White translates, yawning openly, until she spins on her heels and passes into the neighboring office, leaving Martin in his one-on-one with the policeman—superintendent, inspector?—who continues to leaf through the file, and without taking any undue offense, to read each piece of paper one by one, conscientiously, attentively.

Finally he finishes, and coming back to the first, inquires, with raised eyebrows, as to the truth of the facts related there.

It's true, Martin did say that he isn't a volunteer, but he didn't realize he wasn't supposed to say it, he adds, everybody's been in the know, for quite some time, what difference can it make?

The other doesn't bat an eye, moves on to the second paper. That's true as well, it's harder to hide out in cities, he ought not to have said it either, but who can't imagine such a thing, is it such a secret?

At the third paper, Snow White reappears, plops herself on a corner of the desk, blurts out to Martin: "You're doing quite well without me, I see," lingers all the same, files her nails, all but breaks into humming, Martin thinks, but events take a dramatic turn: air-raid warning, everyone gets up, pandemonium, doors bang, people moving around, shouts, they dash down the hallway.

The inspector calmly emptied the contents of a closet and with utmost simplicity asks Martin to help him, sticks a stack of files into his arms.

Hallways, stairways, stampede to the basements, Martin flabbergasted finds himself in a cellar, files on his lap, Snow White at his side, ten or so men around them sitting quietly, without a word, two dogs in front of the armored door, police dogs, that's certain.

The men are young, in the prime of youth, and the unfortunate foreign worker takes to musing that they are far more peaceful here than at the front, it opens out horizons to him, all this wretched paperwork is a good omen.

The workshop stool pigeon was overzealous, who can he be, it's already old, last year or at the beginning of this one, really went all out, ludicrous words, why bring it back up now, and this scene, in the shelter, this scatterbrained girl, these dogs, it isn't true, these mute stuffy fellows, who's going to break out laughing first?

Snow White pours herself some coffee, stretches out on the bench, falls asleep. Past noon, from time to time the voice rises in the loudspeaker, threat over our city, large enemy squadrons, heavy silence, and if it was serious, Good Lord, what are they going to do with him?

The warning stays in effect, the inspector on the bench opposite stares at him without curiosity, indifferent no doubt, only zealous, what a cushy job, insignificant matters, routine.

And who's been sharpening the bits all this while, production paralyzed, everybody around here could care less, it's really too much all the same, pathetic gossip, a farce, he regains hope.

A little later on is convinced that they're going to leave him there, the end of the raid will sound, they'll all leave, close the armored door upon him, Snow White snickers, he stays with the dogs.

The light will go out, what will happen then, black hole, he dozes off, sleeps, and the end of the raid sounds, two o'clock, everybody goes out, he too, up the stairs lugging his files, the dogs have already gone off, Snow White slips away.

The office once again, and the imperturbable man puts everything back in place, bolts the closet, comes back to his seat and takes up the file again, the sheets, questions.

These groups, these networks, Martin explains, reasons, don't hold up, and what do you expect, Italy, Serbia, the person listening misunderstood, or else mixed up everything when he took his notes, made additions.

To make himself look good, the defendant almost said, who at one moment is ready to burst into laughter, at another thinks things aren't one bit funny, the session going on and on, and he's tired, hungry, thirsty, doesn't know what to think anymore, feels very depressed, rattled, incredulous.

At a certain point, the man flashes a small smile, quickly suppressed. He lingers a long moment studying the file, impenetrable, silent, then closes it plainly and simply, sets it back on the pile, says to Martin that he can go, it's over.

He really knew that it was all just a joke, Martin's sure of it now, and he crosses the fateful threshold in the opposite direction, is back in Karolinenstrasse, stepping hurriedly, provided he's not called back, goes into a pastry shop, orders a big puff cake, goes to eat it over by the river.

Past four o'clock, won't return to the factory this time, beautiful fall weather, the willow branches dip into the water, what a to-do, dead leaves at Trodelmarkt, he made it through quite well.

And what if they're taking out the other file? Have already taken it out perhaps, and have dropped it.

Or else it's not over yet, winter sun already, the war drags on.

The large house, I'm drawing near, enigmatic this way with all the shutters closed, the very high roof with five skylights and the big chimneys in the obtuse angle of the arris, the five windows on the first floor, the four on the ground floor framing the door in the center, shutters and door a dull dark blue, pilasters and perron steps reached through weeds that I haven't cut for a long time, wild lawn up to my knees and this silence, this silence all around, how frightening a sound from inside the house would be.

I walk around it, pass under the large linden overlooking the spot where the pond disappears underground, the water accumulating since the storm, move along the cellars in the forest of nettles and climb the small staircase leading to the courtyard, the grass not as high here, uneven, scorched, I have before me now the back door of the house, climb the two wide steps between the short low wall and the symmetrical pots of the oversized oleanders in disarray, I extend the key toward the lock, anxious about the result, what is going to happen, I turn the key and the flap open, the great coolness of the hallway strikes me, is always striking.

And my fingers grope for the fuse box, throw the switch and the light seems to settle on the colored surfaces rather than flush them out, it happens gently, instantaneousness, disconcertion, surprise that everything is in its place, each object in the state it was left and the musty smell of the furniture, the smell of the last elmwood fire.

Dining room, this faded blue, the diamond-patterned curtains of the alcove, massive volume of the hood on the ashen bricks of the hearth and pitchers, goblets, trays and pewter plates, I pass the glass door opening onto the living room, low armchairs and round tables on the tarnished red of the parquet's strips, in the half-light engravings and drawings on the walls, the time spent here can be calculated in qualities of prints and marks displayed, wood carved under the weight of gesture, museum house of gesture in all its applications, repetitions over so many years of distance traveled, slippages, strikings, jumps and jolts, constraints, obliterations, circumventions, this place fashioned my body more than my body molded it, eroded, warped.

The notebooks on the large table in the study, just as I left them, little dust has accumulated on top, the dictionary opened, I liked for everything to look alive, still in circulation, the shelves awaiting classification in an order I was never able to settle on, I hesitated between several orders and the time for leaving the house of books came too soon.

It's dark in the study and the rectangle of the billiard table looms up in the cone of brightness under the mauve lamp, the balls are there in their triangular figure.

Creaking steps on the stairs, slightly wobbly banister, exact displacements recorded intact in the ankles and knees, implicit programming of the hand as it turns the doorknobs, light switches in the rooms, eyes inspecting closets and beds, guest quarters, and the dark room, walls covered with photos all those years, frozen bodies, and smiles.

The staircase, narrower there, comes up against the trapdoor at the threshold of the immense attic where Bernard used to come to paint in summer. Enormous colonies of bats used to live under the slate roof, in the sunlight, the mothers carrying their young clinging to their bellies, I often saw them, they were pipistrelles I think, perhaps there are still some around today.

Hot grey space under the intersecting beams and the grand intricacy of sharp angles, sunshine stabbing through the skylight panes, webbed by spiders, I draw near and see the other house lower down through the branches, sense the pond hollow, follow the line of small oaks bounding the meadows.

Retreat. Retreat into the attic, along the double flight of the timeworn staircase and the long hallway, visit completed, intimate ritual, with muffled footsteps, I withdraw backwards, respectful of the silence and the faded colors, shut off the electricity, pull the door flap closed, turn the key.

The yard in the waning light, I left the garden chairs out, without gathering them together, some in front of the shed, others under the pigeon house, or even in the orchard, in the lane between the plum and apple trees, what used to be the lane, now scrub, a month from now the fruit will be ripe, I'll mow under the trees.

Low wall of the enclosure indiscernible under the tangle of brambles, making the best kind of enclosure, if "enclosing" had any meaning anymore.

Six o'clock, and I haven't opened the notebook, didn't sit in front of the table, the thought didn't occur to me, it's the first time, I believe.

Couldn't care less either way, something else, this very afternoon, has begun perhaps, it happened just like that, without forcing an effort, it's good that way, without a thought.

The idea that he's going to be called back, reconvened, obsesses him. Whoever walks toward his machine fills him with apprehension regarding unforeseen, indecipherable consequences, nurtured by hilarious, preposterous accounts in which refutation gets contaminated, bogged down.

At other moments, Martin gives it no thought, simply abstains from speaking, grows anxious all the same about what he could have said these last months, what the impassive man over in that place hasn't gotten to yet. Who's the informer here, he asks himself, scrutinizing people's eyes.

Mute workshop, mute booming factory, population laid flat as if still under shock, traumatized, amnesiac perhaps, completely conditioned, day and night, in every place, its unconscious colonized.

Martin's not alone in wondering about this no doubt, how it was able to happen, in being amazed, things moved so quickly, ten or so years, accelerated lately, retreats, defeats, being surrounded.

A new event really, seizing power across the board, in memories, in minds, public life, private life, vitiated outcome of so many battles and conquests, twenty centuries of culture to reach this point, a contortion, regression, soon the nation besieged, asphyxiated, superior race itself tracing the map of its ghetto.

History led astray, vocabulary brought to heel, parody of reason, perversion of grammar and conjugations, rigged use of tenses, expurgated dictionary, impoverishment of the word, banishment of inflections, of polysemous meanings, of nuances.

This degradation of language gradually overcomes him, feels this strongly, vaguely guilty about using it so, reading newspaper texts, speaking in circumlocutions and euphemisms, the exact words would make everybody roll their eyes and burrow back underground.

The affair of the file, the interrogation, mentioned it only to Gunther. Went back over to his place many times, Gunther speaks to him about the city in the past, one of the most open in the country, democratic, tolerant, they promoted it to the party's city, blighted it, did quick work in reversing its image.

Raids by storm troopers, street attacks, lynchings, sacking of the synagogue, its eradication, only an empty lot left today, vacant land by the river, two bushes growing there.

So Martin comes back, one Saturday in November, to the old house with the diamond-shaped half-timbering, he knows the pitfalls well at present, the dark, cramped vestibule, the rickety staircase.

The stove draws just as poorly, the smoke gets to the throat, the windows often must be cracked open. Starry sky this evening, clear night, a tower of the Burg collapsed the other day, and Walpurgiskapelle, hit by countless bombs.

Gunther very excited, he sees the end very near, before Christmas, crazy to get all ensnared, a swift armistice would be the lesser evil, in a few weeks it'll be too late, everything will topple, fall in ruins.

Martin, for his part, doesn't believe this anymore, things will run to the end of their course, launched blind, deaf to the facts of the world, weapons touted as apocalyptic will enter the arena, everything could still be braced for the worst, exacerbated, amid the ruins.

Gunther pictures the last day of the war, the cross will be burned, the camps opened, will he see once again those he knew in that place?

He presses his ear against the door from time to time, listens to the noises on the stairs, refugees from the east have just moved in on the floor below, they see spies everywhere, he's a little suspicious.

After dinner, he brings over a bottle still a quarter full, two small glasses in which he pours raspberry brandy, also brings a screwdriver, which intrigues Martin.

"Wait and see, it's a secret!

"To your health," he adds, mysteriously, and he draws out the pleasure a long moment.

Then he rises and, suddenly serious once more, flips down a corner of the threadbare carpet, kneels on the floor, screwdriver in hand, looks for a place under the dust, and working the tool, removes a parquet strip.

Studies the hiding place a moment, then brings to light a roll of paper, wipes it meticulously, and getting up, sets it on the table in front of Martin.

"Open it up and look."

Martin, incredulous, unrolls the parchment. Appears under his eyes an old-style engraving depicting the city's Masonic Lodge, it's a reception ceremony, or an enthronement, the newly elected member is apparently taking an oath, the dignitaries of the lodge, standing, solemnly lend their ears.

Gunther's name is there, beautifully inscribed under the engraving, his rank given in the hierarchy of the Order, the date also marked down.

Finger on his lips, Gunther listens carefully at the door, then, assuring himself that his friend has taken in the scene, returns to the table and carefully refolds the document, puts it back in its safe place, screws down the strip, pulls up the carpet.

Fills the glasses again and toasts, without saying a word, knows that Martin understands the importance of the moment, the meaning of the event, small ceremony reviving the former, friendship sealed with the secret being removed, in the long deferred display of the object become a precious asset over time, a testimony and relay of hope, text buried under his feet for so many years, with Gothic letters authenticating an almost sacred bond.

Martin listens to this silence, savors it, he sees himself there in the ceiling lamp's conical beam, and the bottles, the glasses on the tablecloth. Gunther very pale, brilliant eyes behind his glasses, the remainder of the room in shadow, latticework of the skylight and sharp angles of the roof beams jutting in the half-light, a chiaroscuro setting for a mute intimate drama in the great local tradition.

And perhaps Gunther mightn't say another word, perpetuating the emotion, absorbed by a cherished reminiscence, but the sirens burst upon him, those of the pre-air-raid warning, shattering the charm, and Martin yanked from his contemplation, fearing that the real air-raid will be sounded before long, immobilizing him in the neighborhood, gets up, grabs his coat, and the light wavers, goes out.

All the lights go out, it's by candlelight that he goes down the stairs, takes leave of Gunther at the doorstep to the street, hastens across the paving stones, all lighting cut off, reaches the island and crosses it, but the air-raid sirens ring out, deafening racket in the lunar light, a clear noise rises in the western skies, the defense cannons spring into action, rattle out.

And runs toward the nearest shelter, Lorenzplatz, dashes in just as the warden bolts the steel door.

Two hours later, past midnight, he approaches the school, stepping along circumspectly, slips into a basement window he spotted recently, leading to one of the building's cellars, falls onto a heap of coal, and going up cautiously, slinking along the walls in the striking silence, reaches on tiptoe the barrack's door.

At each corner of the stairs, a mute statue, pallid under the moonlight, tracks him.

Alone here in the evening, in living memory I'll soon say, striving to vary my menu but without hope, sick to my stomach of canned food, pick up a sausage for tomorrow over at old Lambert's, some salted butter, a smoked ham, he must still keep such things in stock, perhaps the butcher has reappeared, slips away often, where the devil can he be off to that way?

The two soft-boiled eggs in their shells, sprinkled with clear water, the slice of Gruyère from a largely eaten chunk, for dessert the blackberries gathered the other day, and these sour sloes in the thornbushes near the well.

A battalion of living creatures keeps me company, I hear them, don't see them, edging in between the stones, the beams, the walls, creeping through the undergrowth, running through the grass, chewing, gnawing, rats and mice, voles in the prairie, brown rats or field mice, the tiny pointy-nosed shrews, with red teeth, so cruel looking.

Moles in great numbers and hedgehogs, civets, rare weasels, the ermine I saw one winter morning, white in the meadow, very cheerful, leaping from one rock to another.

Foxes, yes them too, I spotted one several years ago, crossing the courtyard, going off at a jog, in no hurry, on his way from the chicken coop, there was still a chicken coop back then.

That was the period of traveling, my "self" scattered across five continents, quest for a place of exile, for an identity, destroyed by the war, childhood shattered by it.

Site of childhood overshadowed, erased, illegible under thick strokes of black ink, letters censored, lamps camouflaged, family ground buried, scoffed at, soiled, long-lasting warquake.

Orphaned prospects, native soil lost where familiar animals could be heard screeching, growling, houses of peace where the child ran, circles drawn in the garden, the magical hours of playtime, this splendor in the grass.

The voyages dictated the tone and the new tempo, distance measured from the old continent, everything was diversified, regenerated in every domain, voyages also meaning what vibrates on page or canvas, screen or barred stave, signs colorfully figured.

Time of research and fervor, original questions looming up, a continuous demand for written, oral facts, in new compound forms, given to be listened to and seen, deciphered, translated, it seemed to be taken for granted, the élan lasted, was strengthened with a new upsurge, there wasn't enough time to know everything.

We pulled up short afterwards, it must be said, excess in the opposite direction, a slackening of tension and nothing happened at all anymore, no more confrontations, debates over ideas, views of the future, statistics drowned everything, percentage of listeners and averages, no violence this time, everything liquidated on the quiet, return to the norms of the past century, stereotypes in demand, assumption of the cliché.

A ground swell, who saw it coming, and here you are back where you started, knights of arms and letters, intoxicated with parodies and pastiches, old-school plagiarism, all invention exceeding the norm mocked, coitus refused, empty pleasure.

At this point, cut off the sound, what point is there in still listening to the voice, untimely nostalgia. To shed a tear over the past, such cozy inanity, old as the world, fanciful spin-off treacherously inserted into the program and digestion strained, the paltry dinner wastes away there.

I move into the bedroom, see the notebook on the table in the corner at the edge near the window, I haven't opened it today, it's true, strange that I gave it no thought this evening, no remorse, no worry.

Break with the ritual, the session didn't take place today, I didn't pull the table in front of the window, didn't sit in the iron chair, didn't take up the traditional posture, grey pencil in my hand, looking evasive, anxious, staring at the leaves of white paper as if, written in mute ink, my work consisted in baring the letters, progressively, very gently, with precise, appropriate touches.

Perhaps this is a turning point, something's got to move one of these days and transform itself; that it happened like this, without forcing an effort, without feeling sorry, is something to be ascribed to perseverance, the days to come will determine whether the glimmer persists.

The sunlight is fading, table and big bed in the shadows, the fireplace hood and the andirons perpendicular on the ashen brick, I close the shutters, cross the hallway and, raising the door curtain, go into the living room. Turn on the electricity.

No light this evening, power cut off.

It had been a long time.

Snowfall and intense cold, the snow smooths out, attenuates the projections of forms, their crevices, cracks. Thus disguised, the city seems still virtually undamaged.

However, an attack has just harmed the suburbs north of the river, bombs exploded around the school, one right upon a shelter, thirty Russians perished, including Big Dimitri who often had fun, at his own risk, haranguing his people from the top of the gallery, mimicking somebody or other.

These are terror bombings, the radio says, we will conquer terror, the newspapers repeat, and Martin notices that, far from sowing panic and discouragement, they're driving people to exasperation, to resist, to steel themselves, and made indignant by the blind harassments, their only thought is for revenge.

If there is any terror, it is experienced in the demand for, and reinforced hope of, revenge; weapons of "reprisal," enormous, undetectable rockets, have caught the enemy off guard very recently, spreading panic, a prelude to a counterattack and decisive final assault.

What could still be saved and spared, cities and treasures, ancient and recent riches, are going to be annihilated, ruined, the contortion, the fanaticism leave him flabbergasted, the same goes for the glory of perishing besieged, delirious, cursing, of liquidating on their own what remained by some miracle intact.

Martin wonders how the movie is coming along, about Kolberg, doesn't hear any more talk about it, are they mobilizing battalions to play the assailants, soon all they'll need to do is film the enemy in person, with no makeup, no special effects, documentary footage versus fiction, the former exemplary, an even more colossal budget, money down the hole, distribution to theaters problematic, they might as well write it off.

Demoralized rather, winter has arrived, the second winter, must renew his shabby, threadbare wardrobe: shirt, coat, socks, warm trousers; coupons for bread, meat, finance the deal, spread out over weeks, insane bartering, but he's had it with shivering in the freezing streets swept by the eastern wind.

From the east also comes the other terror for the subjects of a chancellor who has described that particular enemy as a primate, not even savage, subhuman, and a good many refugees have streamed in lately, some, from Rumania, put up at the school in the cellars, the courtyard, rich peasants with long fur pelisses transporting whole families and supplies, oil and wine no doubt, in big goatskins alongside which, unsociable, contemptuous, quick to threaten, their servants keep watch day and night in the hallways, squatting in the darkness, astrakhan fur hats down over their brows.

As for the factory, it still hasn't been hit, and Martin has no end of sharpening tools, he has picked up some skill at it and his attention sometimes suffers, aided by torpor; most recently, the drill having slipped, the grindstone gashed his right index finger, skin scorched to the bone and the pain came only afterward, the alcohol at the infirmary woke him up for good and he was sent back, with bound dressing, to his machine; the scar traces a furrow in his phalanx, a reminder to be vigilant for the remaining operations.

No news from the inexpressive Krolinenstrasse office man studying his file as if in a dream. He dreamed about it, in fact, many times over, the condensed group of players located the scene in the cellar, the man perched on a barrel. Snow White was biting into an apple and the dogs surrounded Martin.

The novelty in his private life has been the reappearance of the tall brunette from workshop 26, who had lost sight of him during the summer, and worked so hard in getting around him that she succeeded in convincing him to follow her one evening.

Heidi lives in Gastenhof, beyond the Plärrer. All that's left of the three-story house is the ground floor. Collapsed hallway, rubble-strewn dining room, she's withdrawn into two rooms, kitchen and bedroom, that she's caulked as best she can. No more electricity in the neighborhood, an old oil lamp animates the intimate setting.

Heidi's a fine girl, rather pretty, playful, not so tall all things considered, sentimental and lonely, husband killed in Russia two years ago now, dreams of music and a cozy interior, speaks about children too, talks about her childhood in the country.

Lavishes him with attention, puts big rustic cakes into the oven, opens the wood stove full blast, would like him to spend the night.

Martin likes being with her, tenderness and cheerfulness surprise him, simplicity too, the absence of vanity, is sorry he didn't get to know her earlier.

Doesn't dare stay the night, the frequent rounds of the policemen in the barracks dissuade him, he leaves before midnight, goes back by tram to the station, walks the rest of the way and slips in through the basement window; the pile of coal is diminishing, he falls farther and farther, dull crunch, muffled in the school's basement.

The prohibited escapade is going to thicken his file, the brunette duplicates the blond in the recurring dream, the man with the dogs will soon have other things to do than worry about him, he muses, he too will be sent off to defend the soil of the fatherland.

The gentle warmth drives away his fears, the lamp's flame makes their shadows tremble on the walls of the narrow premises hemmed in by snow and chromos of ruins.

Christmas in a matter of days, Heidi is so looking forward to it, a tree is an absolute must, she says, and she takes him off into the forest the following Sunday.

The silence, there, strikes him again, so close to the city, the particular space of this forest, Germanic, legendary, an exclusive property of the ocean, this white, motionless sky, the smell of sand and resin.

The idea of other forests toward the east, steeper, more densely leaved perhaps, and beyond, bare, endless plains, with scarcely an undulation. Central Europe, the threshold, he repeats, wholly absorbed by his feeling. Space without drama, or event, within the imminence of event.

Heidi was born over there, she points, right before the mountains, doesn't understand what fable he's spinning out, it's her own country, the soil of his story, exotic or not.

A geographic feeling, yes, language submits to the body in its orientations, élans and safeguards, apprehensions, showy displays.

Body linked with the elements, through earth and rock, the state of the sky, the wind.

The weight of snow here, Heidi, and the even light in the straight cuttings at the crosspaths, receding skyline, poorly defined.

The sky's capsizing over there, don't you see—an eclipse?

Surprising that I've never been stricken by panic here, isolated as I am, without weapons, nor any hope for help, I'd shout myself hoarse to no purpose, nobody would come running, they'd step slowly closer, surround me, a real death trap.

A simple matter to climb to the windows if you're not afraid of nettles, the door itself, despite its two bolts . . . But no, I fall asleep peacefully, naked under the sheet as always, often threw it off lately, until the storm.

Daylight rims the curtains, awakens me, I often spend a long moment scrutinizing the space of the room, verifying its qualities, the space of the dream that has just ended endures and disturbs it, and the mournful voices inhabiting it.

I don't like staying in bed, once my eyes are opened; as soon as I'm up, everything falls back into place, marks and points of reference, the planned agenda, the state of things, of my ideas on the question, if I may be so bold.

Big fears in the past, sudden, insurmountable, I barricaded myself in, ran from one window to another, certain that the prowler had already slipped inside the house, threaded his way up the stairs, was lying in ambush behind an upstairs door or crouched in the attic, biding his time.

A harmless noise triggered the alarm, those cracks and bangs that can be heard at all times, the alarm arises from a meeting, between noise and intimate voice, between voice and intimate voice, between traces of places, faraway and with no point in common, drawing toward each other in the darkness of their dwelling and brushing close, then steering clear of one another.

That I experience nothing more of the sort here can be ascribed to the cramped space, I believe, to its simplicity, to this regrouping of all functions on one level, or else something has really transformed itself in the distribution and preservation of traces, or the majority of traces are erased, become inoffensive, devitalized in a way.

I may well have lost my emotivity, my sensibility perhaps. Like those people in the village? Overcome like them by apathy, without noticing? Is this a flash of insight, burst of lucidity, reprieve or warning?

What suave, underhand work on the subject, in order to make it compatible—nerves and muscles, gaze, understanding, elocution—with the new order?

Silence. Great silence all around, the silence of men, birds, everywhere weeds, sunken lanes become footpaths, dismantled fences, livestock evacuated a long while ago, slaughtered no doubt, or dead of hunger, carcasses in the meadows, scrap metal of cars abandoned there, frames of skeletons rising in the scrub, farms and barns in ruins, or else incinerated, pillaged.

The heat returns, everything is dry once again. The only visible effect of the downpour, the pond level, up to the low wall yesterday, the grasses are going to turn green again, the ones I call "lettuces" or "watercress," stringy algae that the excess chemical fertilizer caused to proliferate, they ought to have disappeared over time, in sum dying by inches.

I open the windows wide in the three rooms, model bachelor quarters in that bygone world, pied-à-terre in the country, privileged, still preserved, a rustic if not comfortable residence, comfortable if not charming.

Supplies for a few weeks, assured short-term safeguard, and this matter of the vegetable garden, or chicken coop, that's dragging on, wardrobe worn thin, threadbare, worn through but no matter, the only alarming thing is the state of my sandals, shoes, boots, go over to the village and see if I can't swap them for a good bottle, a new pair of ankle boots.

Sunshine this morning, clear sky, breakfast on the terrace, always the best meal of the day, the most satisfying, reinvigorating, light.

Power cut, rare at this hour, rare since the big outage in February, a week without electricity, I tried reading by candlelight in the evening, Gothic novels, comic books, went to bed early, casting a distressed eye upon the cassette shelf.

A few steps on the path in front of the terrace, I ought to mow the grass one of these days, the bush is taking possession of the countryside, absorbing the bumps, canceling out or attenuating the differences in level, substance, color.

It's spreading over every surface, in every direction, assaults the stones of the house, pulls them free, yanks them up as I saw once in a tropical jungle, in America I believe.

Roots raising monuments, clutching the enormous blocks, attracting and destabilizing them, covering them over, imprisoning, disintegrating.

Muscles of chlorophyll, plant tentacles, arms of the jungle versus human hands.

And how does man measure up against all this?

Garlands on Königsstrasse, rare pines at the intersections, people collecting for the Winter Aid Society trudge through the mud, a halo of festivities as if prerecorded during cold weather: not scenes so much as glimpses or performances from years past, visions, images with no interconnection, memory already betrays.

The traces will interlink with others, imprinted under other skies, safeguarded from childhood, from adolescence, tales told by others, passages from novels whose aging characters endlessly pace about their rooms, mixing up their memories, confusing everything.

On New Year's Eve, Martin over at Heidi's let the time go by, no more trams after midnight, remained until daylight, and morning. In the afternoon, at the movies, they saw a melodrama in which the musician hero, a highly skilled pianist, struck his chords like one possessed, windows open on the storm, drowning his keyboard in tears.

The day after New Year's, the unfathomable boredom of the factory routine and the throbbing dizziness, broken by the burning reminder of the brief instant when the grindstone countersank his finger; the mark is there, clearly visible, he'll easily identify it later on, more rapidly than those inscribed only

God knows how in what's called "memory."

Return to the camp after nightfall, Jitomir no longer displays the same high spirits as before the men died in the shelter, he was in there too, came out without his voice, miraculously, half suffocated.

Cheerless evening in the white light and racket, jokes about his little jaunts fall flat, Martin goes to bed early, is in a deep sleep no doubt when the air-raid siren goes off, the others up already, running through the galleries, only enough time for him to get dressed, the cannons thunder, dashes down the stairs among the very last.

The same old recurrent episode of indefinite waiting in the half-darkness, the thick steel door dangerously shaken when a bomb falls nearby, visibly wobbling, buckling, on the point of breaking open; once, in a factory shelter, Martin wound up with the Ukrainian girls, some had their whole bodies shaking, eyes riveted on the door, their self-control gone, muttering prayers.

The planes can be heard, a clear and massive humming, hundreds probably, the defense cannons ring out in the foreground, no bombs yet it seems, no sustained vibration of the door, the ground not markedly trembling, nor any sudden influx of that mute, brutal breath that somehow violates the locale's confined air and flattens the nape, cuts off breathing, tosses the body to the side.

No idle chatter in the shelter, never, each person remains silent, listens or falls asleep, dozes, keeps his eyes peeled, watches the signs, goes over his fears or his indifference, his unconsciousness perhaps, but doesn't speak a word, doesn't whisper, the shelter warden by the radio receiver keeps motionless watch, the sound crackles in the set, at irregular intervals the nasal voice comes through with an update, ever cautious, neutral, as if the matter were of no personal concern, confirms for the moment that the pressure isn't letting up, other formations are approaching, are going to fly over the city.

Then the light suddenly goes out, a flashlight snaps on near the entrance, still no explosions, or else they're very far away, a half hour already, Martin is about to doze off, the dry heat tasting of oil and metal gets to him as much as the uncomfortable bench, he rises to his feet, leans back against the cement pillar, moves his legs, forces himself to observe his companions in captivity through the restless, fitful glimmer, to become attached to details, to react, in a word, and pass the time.

The odor alerts his nostrils, he had no doubt been picking it up for several minutes, but he suddenly identifies it, a light veil of smoke, a trace in this part of the shelter, just here perhaps, no alarm seems to be spreading over there.

The radio has been silent for a while now and the warden, anxious in turn, draws near the door, sniffs, coughs, looks at his watch, soon it'll be an hour since the raid began, speaks in hushed tones, as if undecided, puzzled.

Now the smoke slowly invades the cellar, progressively filling it, appears to pour in from all sides, several people in discussion over there, moving about, no more orders over the radio, no more news, the sound still crackles but the set is mute, seemingly deserted, abandoned, or else the man sits voiceless before the microphone, incapable of speaking, of articulating a sound.

The bitter fumes get into the throat, sting the eyes, groans and coughing fits, each man protects himself as best he can, holds his breath, someone in a hoarse voice begs the man in charge to unblock the door, to clear the exit, the other seemed to have been waiting for the signal, raises the steel arms, pulls the heavy door toward him and all light vanishes, the dense cloud rolls in.

Elbow to elbow gasping in the suffocating darkness, Martin stumbles on a rock, falls to his knees, finds the staircase finally and sees the glimmer on the wall, then the flame on the roof, flames on the galleries.

Emerges into the hallway on the ground floor, reaches the vestibule running amid the interplay of quivering shadows and the rain of flying sparks, passes the porchway and finds himself in the middle of the street, stops short.

Opposite, the houses are burning, the whole street is burning, in the near silence, no sound but the gentle crackling everywhere on the roofs, the dull thud of a beam, the hissing of flames in the wind, everywhere a violent wind.

Between the paving, incendiary tracers have lodged sideways, the stone blackens in the sizzling phosphorus, Martin advances to the corner of the building and along Neudorferstrasse sees the neighborhoods burning on the hills on the other side of the river, a gigantic inferno looming westward.

He stands there shattered, emotionless, not even incredulous, mindful of this gap inside, sees himself at the intersection of two streets, observing, listening.

The city blaze doesn't make much noise, very unexpectedly, he'd never have imagined such a thing, the whole city is burning, as far as the eye can see, and he hears nothing but the sound of the wind.

Bike rusted but that's just too bad, should take better care of it, keep it up, I have everything I need, oilcan, paint, special liquid for the chrome, it's like the vegetable garden, as long as I'm not forced to I won't, only in dire straits, I who am so responsible, so strict about other things.

Basket on the luggage rack, I'm off now, no problem until reaching the road, at which point the potholes, the pebbles strewn on what's left of the tar, the slope steepening in the *causse*, it's really rare for me to reach the hilltop without getting off, and what difference can it make whether I arrive up there on foot or bike, nobody around to tell me that I've gotten weaker, that I'm not what I used to be.

These city dwellers' shacks that had proliferated on the hill after the war, with menhir in the garden and old stones, brought back, swiped from the wayside crosses, not much left of them today, cheap constructions, crumbled roofs, breeze-block under the nettles, menhirs sticking out askew from the brambles.

I get back on my bike, caution at the curves on the road down, if my single brake were to give way, enter the village discreetly, moving at a slow pace, zigzagging, town hall burnt down to the left, to the right bistro in ruins, and then the war memorial, the big puddle of water at the intersection.

The single street deserted, as usual, neither dog nor cat, hope that old Lambert's around; I part the curtain at the doorstep to the shop, yes he's there, or his shadow, totally stupefied, drowsy, can hardly move this morning.

Latest village news, nothing new, no more power, asks if I've any at my place, what a question, takes a lot of coaxing for the sausage, no more ham at any rate, he assures me, he repeats it as if perversely delighted, no more salted butter, no more anything.

Shoes? Doesn't even have any for himself, shows me his clogs; I mention the good bottle, he's going to work it out, see what he can do, a little more alert all of a sudden, begins to tell me a muddled story, about boots, ankle or hobnailed, babbles, relights his butt, I leave him there, cross the street.

The baker woman is out of sorts, asks for aspirin, aspirin or syrup, has a heartrending cough, the next time, yes certainly, she depresses me, very depressing all those who've remained, and those who've left, what state are they in? Where are they, what are they doing, nobody ever wrote, nor called, no postcards, neither beach nor snow, no New Year's greetings.

The butcher's been back, for some while, deafer than ever, constantly smiles, a mysterious air, places a finger on his lips, goes into the back of the shop, returns with a cutlet wrapped in a beautiful piece of blackish-brown paper as in the old days; promises me one every week, it's well worth a pack of shag, it's a promise.

For the shoes I write on a sheet of paper, as usual, two very simple sentences, in which shoes and cognac counterbalance each other to perfection, economically and grammatically, subject, verb, complement.

Big smile presides over the reading, over his embarrassed

expression when he tells me that he doesn't grasp, can't manage to read, that's something new, is he poking fun at me?

No, he still deciphers, articulates the syllables, but the words don't make sense anymore, seem to have lost their meaning, become interchangeable, or a matter of pure decorative charm, design, sound spectacle, futile, he apologizes, stupidly.

Disconcerted, I make myself understood with gestures, he says he's going to look, doesn't leave me much hope, displays his slippers, down at the heels, worn through soles.

I run to the post office and push my paper under Madame Paule's nose. "Oh, you too?" she says. "The pastor came to see me yesterday, very disturbed, bothered, missal in hand, can't manage to read it anymore, it's beyond him, he doesn't understand a word."

We started laughing but really there was nothing funny. Doesn't make a big deal about it, she blames it on his age, is surprised I take everything so tragically, that I make such a great fuss.

No mail, obviously, I went home the same way, riding half the time, the other on foot, very perturbed, even anxious, missed the turn at the bottom of the slope.

Ran to the living room, picked up the first book I fell upon, Fénelon, opened it and began reading at random.

Read two pages, three, very normally, nothing changed, with great pleasure even, every sentence kept its weight, its tone, its color.

Every line kept its meaning, every sign, every element. It's not the same meaning as before, however, before the incidents, it's something different.

Every word means something and this meaning appears distant, obsolete, from another age.

Superfluous perhaps, and refined, luxurious!

The old city burned down, a portion of the suburbs, some are still burning a month afterward, the flames can be seen on the hills to the north a month later.

Martin strolls between the standing ruins, walking along the streets turned into footpaths or muddy creeks between the banks of rubble perfunctorily cleared away and the deep excavations, gaping cellars, craters, tumulus of buildings crumbled like ancient dry-stone huts—you can see very far now, on both sides of the river, very far in the valley, the city has become a valley again, slopes out in the open, and its meanderings, banks—Martin has the feeling of a perfect climax, it couldn't be any other way in the end, this is the real end, everything was pointing to it from the beginning, signified it with veiled words, the long delay was a deferment, procrastination, postponement, the real one comes now, at the end of the war.

Often in the evening he goes for a walk and seeks out the places, with eye and ear, in his legs reliving the traces of yesterday's gait, reexperiencing the sensations of yesteryear, emotions, ensemble impressions, when he used to enter along Marientor and Lorenzstrasse in the summer and reach the main square by one or the other bridge.

He had a vision once, a hallucination, had seen the city incinerated, razed, a swift vision, from the top of the Burg, he thinks he remembers. Scanning the dead city today, he fails to picture in his mind how he was before, how he lived there, what it looked like before, not so very long ago.

Stops on the museum bridge at times, leans his elbows on the parapet, vainly attempts to imagine the willows and the old facades, the sloping roofs and the skylights, the flowers; the plate remains blurred, nothing reveals itself anymore, phosphorus fragments have burnt the image.

He sought out Gunther's house and didn't find it amid the street rubble; sought Heidi's house and didn't really recognize it. Gunther didn't come back to the factory, Heidi neither, they didn't reappear, are perhaps injured and hospitalized, or evacuated, two thousand people perished they say, one hundred thousand homeless.

Returning from his expeditions on unsteady feet, Martin walks up toward the train station along the narrow alley that once used to be Königsstrasse, accompanied by the heavy odor of cold ash and cadavers.

Those living in the camp were transferred to barracks in the suburbs, just the time it took to repair the damage, barely two weeks and they arrived back in the school, what's left of it on one-and-a-half floors, as best they can cram into the rooms caulked in a slapdash manner, bedsteads pushed even closer together, in the cellars too and even on the galleries, exposed to the wind.

The old city is destroyed, a large part of the suburbs, but the factory is standing, intact, still working, nothing has changed, nothing has stopped working.

Martin found himself transferred to a new job, no more grindstones, bits and drills, he's on a circular machine at present, driven by a steady, stop-start rotation, feeds it with tiny steel cylinders, one every two seconds, feeds several boxes in a row, in rapid bursts of sorts, then sits a second, feeds once again, keeps an eye on the regular cooling of the mechanism, feeds, sits down again.

The foreman is an engineer, he visits the machine, he's the one who thought it up and started it going, questions Martin on its performance, its quirks, it gets stuck now and then.

Fischer's his name, he's very skinny, pale face, sunken eyes, he lost his whole family in the bombing, wife, five children, he's alone at present, in his exhaustion, distraction, delirium, glorifies his country, its strength, its courage, backed by evidence, calls on Martin to witness.

They're alone against everyone, he declares, eyes flashing, very excited, fanatical, the whole world is against us, it takes the whole world together to quash us, to bow us down. Martin found the perfect answer at last: and Japan, he says at a certain point. The other man stops short, looks at him dumbfounded: yes, Japan, it's true, stays there, arms dangling, then turns on his heels, goes off, shoulders hunched over, shaking his head.

Martin knows that he comes back at night, works at night too, doesn't sleep, fascinated with nothingness, extremism, ruin, the catastrophe possesses him and the conflagration, the fire inhabits, nourishes him.

Spiritual flame, the spirit lives within him, no doubt, the famous Spirit, innate Power unifying and encouraging, ascribing, obliging, lives within its culmination and war consumption, in its decline as well, rambling, bewildered, one devil of a paranoia.

A levy en masse is ordered, a people's assault, evenings and Sundays, elderly men, in overcoats and scarves, can be seen maneuvering picks and shovels, women, "armored fists," and children, submachine guns and rifles.

The film progresses likewise in its faithful recreation, unpaid extras of the period, mise-en-scène that's hasty, improvised, thrown together.

One movie house is still open, very far from the center, the single building saved in the neighborhood, shows a black-and-white comedy, familiar '30s stars, light banter, white telephones, Martin goes over one evening, meets his fellow countryman, Mathieu, whom he bumped into once or twice already, at a restaurant, the movies.

Mathieu lives in another camp, north of the city, has decided to leave, take the chance, now's the time, he says, mustn't delay any longer, hesitates to go off, doesn't speak the language well, is looking for somebody to join the venture.

Martin says he's ready, ready to be off as well, in a week or two, he wants to wait a little longer, the other'll wait, he agrees, they'll see each other again some evening soon.

Martin wonders why, that particular night, why he said that, to wait a little longer, for what reason, is surprised, if his mind's made up at last, why hem and haw, postpone the departure?

Wait a little longer, for Gunther to come back, and Heidi, see them one last time, tell them good-bye, perhaps, he doesn't know.

Neither fear of the unexpected nor of failing, he can't come up with an answer, the idea of leaving the city as well, the idea that he's leaving behind a great deal in this city, a year or more of his life, he's not yet twenty, doesn't understand very well, it's beyond him.

The other man's right, surely, is older than he is anyway, more mature, that's certain. So, why not tomorrow?

A long walk to pick myself up, village blues, demoralized every time after getting back, no stopping it, I've already mentioned this, anything can be done to them, they show a little surprise in the beginning then get used to it, neither revolt nor questions, nor recriminations, resignation is another issue, you know what you're resigned to, here people don't know, don't see, don't speak, don't think.

Decline, decay. This accelerated regression makes me shudder, especially when I go to the village it seems to me, the rest of the time I'm unaware perhaps, I too will get used to it, one day.

Degradation of the language and perversion of the game, diversion of words, deprivation of meaning—by violence in the past, by gentleness these recent years, the parallel gains in force at times, a half-century distant.

This thing which is dying out, disappearing, this fading fire, this evening and morning horizon, familiar, fencing in the site, this valorous tenacious harmony, landscape and painting, bonds of book and tales—the sharp impression grows diluted, discolored and the shadows spread, the couch grass.

To have done with the year 2000, a slogan.

Softened sunlight, humid heat once again, the pond gone back to its former dimensions, shallow puddle with coppery glints.

Left after lunch on the path leading to the farm with the dog, a gap in the savannah, I took the sickle, it's safer.

It helps knowing that the well is there, in old Giverne's field to the right: brickwork, tiles, zinc foil and pulley, everything is buried or practically, can be made out, dismantled, between high grass and vines, an impression of being in Mexico.

From here the farm could be seen. At one time. The red roofs between the foliage upon this cambered ground on the other side of the village, barely a hill, parallel to the national highway, about a half a mile farther away, between its poplars that must surely be sheltering it at present.

I know the path, fortunately, the mulberry bushes obstruct it, it's an expedition, pruning it on the right and left, one hundred yards before the farm there was a two-horsepower car trapped in the brambles already, I'd photographed it once.

All the photos in the lab, up there, I'll go pick them up one day, file them, look at them in the afternoons, every subject, every detail, to get some idea, reconstruct the impressions, the emotions, I end up by now knowing anymore, how it was before, how people lived, everyone such as we were, between large and small houses, the sensations, voices, memories we had already, of the time before, the life before, on and on.

At any rate not much choice left if the power doesn't come back on, go for the old photos, date them if they haven't already been, by means of deduction, comparison, annotating them on the back, in short an identification sheet, ages, names, circumstances of the meeting, plus two or three lines of commentary, good composition exercise, strict constraints, providing I've some memory of the surroundings, the atmosphere, I haven't forgotten everything all the same.

My camera is still there, I'd like to take photographs, really should in fact, perhaps alone in thinking about such a thing at this moment, great interest later on, unique documents, roads and villages in this state, population, vegetation, who would have suspected, just take a look, it's incredible, everything was halted, blocked, back at that time, so few stories, we have these photos at least, priceless, I'd sell them for a small fortune if I'm still here, too bad there's no more film to be found anywhere.

Make drawings, for want of that. The pond, old Lambert, his ghostly face, the large closed-up house, the fields. Self-portrait in front of a three-sided mirror, the two profiles, this shaggy beard that's not greying, disheveled shock of hair, all these wrinkles.

Draw myself zigzagging forward on the farm path, machete in hand, emerging onto the turn by the shed, that's the point where the dog burst out, bolted up to us, barking, sniffing, then let us go by, circling or following us along the edge of the ditch, at a jog trot, muzzle to the ground.

Accompanied us as far as the tobacco field, then grew tired, backtracked, letting us continue on in peace. As far as Plane at times, when we were in top form, on beautiful summer days, days like today for example, but today I won't be going, it's too risky.

The road barred by tree trunks and all those mangy dogs out there, silent, threatening, seem to defend a taboo place, stand guard over a treasure or who knows what, things almost turned nasty the last time.

Fence yanked up at the courtyard entrance, main living quarters in the back, doors and windows torn off, thistles everywhere, it used to be a beautiful farm, well maintained, with a pleasing appearance, they'd pass through our place most often on their way to the village, the Gautiers, good farmers, fine people.

From the top of the hill I spot the house, the only inhabited point for far around, the blue-tinted roof barely sticks above the line of foliage, what will I do when the time comes when he'll surrender as well, and the walls will crack, the fireplaces crumble, and the skylights, tiles and stones tumble all around, pile up in the scrub? Leave in turn? What's holding me back then?

Everything a person leaves in a place, all the traces, these things remain, and my body goes off wandering, going back over the gestures and journeys, aimlessly, calling, turning, ceaselessly, without rest.

Sleepless. In the darkness. The moon cuts into the disc of the sun and darkness comes.

Each new day reaches an end and Martin still hasn't gone through with it. He saw Mathieu again at the appointed time, asked him to wait a little longer. Perhaps he's afraid, no matter what he says.

Despite the destruction and a certain disorganization in services, everywhere order reigns, discipline hasn't grown slack, no public sign of weakening or resignation, even less of protest. What chance would there be in getting past the check points?

Gunther and Heidi missing, still reported missing. With work worsened by the lack of rest, Martin comes back to sleep at the factory, in a basement recess where he found a mattress, doesn't sleep well there, the odor of cast iron and concrete gives him a migraine, but it's better than back in the camp, the overcrowded barracks dooms sleep.

The fortress is cracking, ramparts shaken, towers taken by storm, the ditches have been hit, the Vistula, the Danube, the Rhine. Repeated air-raid warnings, day and night, betray the sudden proximity of the front, brief wearing harassments.

One evening while wandering on the heights toward the Burg, fascinated by the spectacle as if a feature still escaped him, one that concerned him intimately, and that he senses will apparently remain hidden a long time perhaps, Martin surprised by the sirens takes off running for the bridge, passes the bridge as the first bombs explode, turning over the ruins, gets back on his way toward Königstor, the only shelter still intact, and is hurled to the ground, hardly hears the noise, hurled violently, flattened, dazed, stones tumbling all around him.

Gets up, staggering, out of breath reaches the shelter, pounds with his fist against the door, a shower of red shoots up in front of the train station, when they finally open for him he's not really aware of what he's doing anymore, what situation he's in, his legs tremble, and his hands, his lips, his whole body.

Realizes he's afraid, that he knows what fear is all of a sudden, never was afraid before then, understands it now, thought in his heart of hearts that he was out of range, never thought he could die there, plain and simple, just like that, his youth doesn't protect him, no more heavenly blessing, he's not immortal, knows it at last, a close call, he almost had it.

Two days later, in Laufertor, with Mathieu he settles on the details of the departure. Everything is very simple from now on, goes very quickly, they'll leave the very next day.

Last factory day in a state of disbelief, a certain unconsciousness, he put a few things in a leather briefcase, all Germans travel with leather briefcases or backpacks, he thinks he's being watched, denounced, spotted, nothing special comes up, nobody follows him to the train station, there he meets up with Mathieu at the fixed time.

Buys the tickets, heading south so they agreed, the first city on the Danube, the train is a local, jam-packed, empties out rather quickly, people going home to suburban towns.

They go up a valley, after dark, patches of snow on the ballasts between the rows of pine trees, Mathieu placid, untalkative as usual with him, repeatedly smiling at the corner of his lips but it's a tic, Martin as if dazed, dozing, doesn't understand too well, then the cold grips him, at once gets a true picture of the situation, it's absurd, what they're up to, they won't get far, to reach Switzerland, the border, with no idea of an itinerary, which way to pass, a mythic ambition, it's madness.

The car all to themselves at present, Martin listens, doors banging, footsteps, readies a sentence if the need arises, an alibi of few words, they're going to a friend's, coming back tomorrow morning, no safe-conduct pass of course, how to explain that, his mind a blank.

Wheezing train, stops for a long time at the small stations, turn-of-the-century railroad, very old villages, snow covers the hills, these are the Jura of Franconia, Mathieu has fallen asleep, for him nothing seems to pose a problem.

He's the one who shakes Martin much later, the train has stopped, lights on the platform, end of the line, the few travelers hasten toward the exit, eleven o'clock, nobody in the waiting room, no ticket collector, the station seems isolated far from the city, Donauworth down below perhaps, the forest nearby, Mathieu leads him along, they go up along a muddy path, no more snow here, very sharp cold.

They leave the path and climb between the trees, halt in a wind-sheltered hollow, Mathieu takes some bread out of his bag, boiled sweet potatoes, they eat a few of them, a bit of bread, Martin thinks that they've finally gotten there, they must have covered approximately sixty miles, better than nothing, how to sleep in a cold such as this, there's no more sleep at present.

Silence in the forest, starry sky, the pale light reassures him, tomorrow they'll go down to the station, ask for tickets to the next stop, everything will go smoothly, no reason not to, a dearth of policemen, with other things to do than conduct trains.

Thinks in vain about the school, the factory, the city, unable to fix them in thought, they drift, between full and empty content, have no more meaning, the eighteen months spent there fall short of language, neutralized sensations, traces confiscated, repressed, stolen on the sly.

Memory on the run, bereaved awakening.

Come back along the stream after the well, hewing my way through the brambles on the culvert and the low wall, through the nettles on the cracked clay, perfectly dry once more and crumbling underfoot, going up in dust. I like this spot very much, this opening into the pond between copse and large trees, elms and chestnuts, the old elms are dying.

Chop them down before winter, plant ashes in their place, willows, more chestnuts. Bald cypresses in the water. Reinforce the banks, acacias on the banks too. In a month at most the pond will be filled, I'll come back in the morning, set myself up on the folding stool and draw the weeds, stumps, dead branches.

The creatures, along the running water, the salamander with the green spots and thin red stripe down its whole body, the grass snake swimming on the surface, the coronillas at the bottom, the viperine snake at the edge of the water, on the loose soil and moss.

I saw a muskrat swimming, once, its long tail like a vertical oar, very quickly, head out of the water, I mistook it for a fish; the moorhens have been gone for years, in the past a couple were nesting on the willows lying in the water, in front of the small house, in the sunlight; one stormy day, the cock raised the nest upon twigs of reeds, outstripping the elements, battling feverishly.

The sun's rays sinking over the *causse* strike the scorched tufts slantwise, the pink ocher clay marquetry, the leaves of the bushes touching the loose stones of the bank and the dense hedge of couch grass, a scythe would be needed to climb that way, going around the pond, and opening a path to the large linden, I take off my sandals and walk into the shallow water, the ground is still firm, reach the gate at the entrance of the swallow hole, scale the low wall.

Beautiful summer evening, so calm in its vegetable torpor and continual absence of wind, unconditional calm, birds flown far off or fallen mute, respecting the proper balance in the off-season, the world in a state of silent suspension.

I go back up toward the house, drops of blood on my shirt, a gash in my left hand, brambles or sickle, cut across the lawn, raise my eyes and see him, see him appear before me there on the path, has been there surely for a while already but coming into sight only at this present moment, from head to foot, fully blown as if through a bid for power and instantly integrated into the landscape, neutralizing the idea of time in the landscape, perhaps even the idea of place.

Red hair, bony, very skinny and tall, jacket and trousers in tatters, planted firmly on his legs looking at me, ten yards away, absolutely motionless, as if there were nothing extraordinary about him being there, putting in an appearance, staring at me, or looking beyond me, staring at the pond, the pool of water glittering in the sunlight or the large house behind the linden, as immobile as the tree, shut up as it is and mute, watchful, on guard.

I must have remained fixed to the spot for a while in turn, pondering, as if recapitulating my trip, the path traced by my steps, and establishing a relationship between these tracks and the abrupt fact of the gazing eyes, seeking a relationship, I wonder why, to find out whether he'd seen me for a long while perhaps, or followed me, preceded me rather, a relationship of gaits, a feature common to the journeys, something is linked to the total number of steps in this matter, the circuit of the itineraries, I don't know, once I set off again the relationship doesn't matter anymore, no longer inevitably posing the supposition that it was ever really imposed, and I draw near, he still doesn't move, he's carrying a bundle at the end of a stick over his right shoulder exactly as in old-fashioned engravings.

I'm a few steps from him, he makes a barely perceptible movement of his head, a greeting perhaps, and I see his eyes, quite asymmetrical, more precisely the left one twitches very quickly, intermittently, never really blinking.

He's right in the middle of the path, I must turn off through the tall weeds if I want to get to the door, he looks at the small house, the door, nods his head again.

Bluish cheeks, ears sticking out, lips partly opened, directs his eyes upon me again, studies me as if I weren't in keeping with the place, yes indeed, more surprised than myself, finding somebody in such a place, mustn't have come upon much of anyone on his road, wherever he comes from.

I formulated the question no doubt, or else it's the first question popped into my mind at any rate, in present circumstances at least. He stretches his arm eastward, southeastward, the farm with the dog, and beyond Villeneuve, quite a hike already, but the arm keeps moving about, pointing out, evoking, naming other horizons, even more distant, more far off on the plateaus to the east.

If he wants to go in, I gesture, to eat, or drink, he can stay if he wants, sleep if he wants, he looks at me attentively, the eye blinks this time, straight out, remains there as if not believing his eyes and he begins to laugh, it's a laugh surely, lips baring his teeth and a spasmodic chuckle shakes him, expressionless he stares at me, movement of his head as if nodding, it's the house he's staring at, through me, choked off chuckling, he turns away, starts walking, has clearly set off again, draws off along the dirt path toward the road, takes slow but long strides, his bundle rocking at the end of his stick, in rhythm, doesn't turn around, arrives at the road and looks toward the village but doesn't hesitate, crosses and continues straight ahead, the *causse* path, continues into the distance with the same step, exit at the bend of the path, suddenly he's out of sight.

Could catch up with him, hold him back. He's leaving, left from where, since when. Leaves his country, goes away. Gives the impression of going away, of knowing where he's headed.

Could fill a bag rapidly, and join up with him, join him, his project, his idea if he's got one, or his absence of any ideas, desires, likings.

Eyes on the path. Will he come back in sight, peopling the setting once again, see if I'm coming?

Give a sign, no. He won't give a sign.

Forest numbingly cold in the first light of morning, freezing dawn, sleep and chill divided the night, they warm themselves as best they can, feet frozen, hands frozen, nibble at the paltry food.

Dare not go down to the station before seven. The waiting room is jammed, service to Augsburg cut off, Augsburg bombed, the only train announced is for Ulm, at nine.

Dare not go down into the city to have a cup of coffee, nor stay in the station. They go off walking in the woods, what's necessary is to keep moving, not to get noticed, not to get nabbed as lazy, idle.

The train is another local. Goes up the valley but nothing much can be seen, the Danube hidden, horizon blocked, at several points crews repairing the damaged tracks, volunteers apparently, not very skilled, frequent, prolonged stops, repetitive scenes, a brilliant precise daylight illuminates the actors.

Overcrowded wagon, people squeezed onto the seats, the stowaways don't talk to each other, answer as little as possible, pretend to be dozing and doze for real, by noon they haven't covered much ground, stuck there in the broad daylight, starving, numb, with no possibility for sneaking away nor flight.

Muddy, devastated banks of an ancestral river, states, famous principalities, ancient country in the heart of Europe, modern war has struck it, ravages it presently, who would have believed this only five years ago, they carried it far away, this war, far outside, far from the borders, for an empire that would last a thousand years.

Autopsy of a disaster, backfire, the people here watch without understanding, speechless with disbelief, as if just awoken, they would really like to stop everything but the train moves forward, and worse, toward the front, five o'clock, Ulm is in sight, it's burning, the train comes to a standstill in a waste ground, they reach the station on foot, it's burning.

Martin, Mathieu tread ground, stride over the debris, cathedral spared in the center of the raging flames, think to themselves their escape comes to an end here, would keep going on foot, but where, in which direction, across fields, they're dying of thirst, wandering aimlessly until evening, nobody worries about them, night is falling when three old cars are assembled on a remote track, scheduled for Memmingen, directly south, time not yet fixed.

Wooden passenger cars, windows shattered, some travelers fill seats after some time, no light, the ghost train sets off after midnight, rides the whole night long, at a crawl, stops twenty times in open country, stretched out on the seats the fugitives paralyzed with cramps see dawn breaking over a canal, a river.

Memmingen in early morning, seems intact, they finally get

something hot to drink at the station buffet, eat a little, Martin penalized by an ugly beard goes off to shave in the washrooms, Mathieu buys the tickets for the following stop, same course as always, Kempten, paces at the end of the platform.

Closely shaven, completely refreshed, Martin comes out of the washroom perked up, towel in hand, and doesn't go any farther, two policemen stop him, those who have an oval plate at the end of a steel chain indicating their duties and position.

No safe-conduct, no pass, Martin leaving the platform solidly flanked sees Mathieu over there watching him without flinching, helpless.

Crossing through the small town, baroque, decked out with flowers, the police station looks out on the main street, everybody turns around at them, Martin disturbed, furious, the policemen leave him in the hands of an inspector who seems empty-handed, examining this trivial case will keep him busy all morning long.

The offender has already trotted out his part of the dialogue, factory destroyed, camp evacuated, I was told to go look for another post in the south, you can call the factory to verify the story, Martin betting that communications have been disrupted, or cut off, or that the factory has been hit after all, seriously.

Suspense, the inspector calls, calls in vain, calls again, perplexed, no connection, at a loss as to what to do with his prisoner no doubt, leaves him stranded for a good two hours then reappears, very satisfied, found him a new position, on the railroad, a small station in the region.

And that very evening, escorted by a police officer, Martin finds himself in a train again, very tired, riding eastward this time, then northward, turning in circles it seems, completely distracted from his fictitious trip, this is Swabia, Bavarian side, he won't be leaving Bavaria, indeed.

Arrives at his destination in a tiny station, a genuine glade in the forest, tortuous path leads to the village dominated by a high castle, circular towers, walls burnished by sunset, that's where he's conducted, worn out, barely surprised.

The forester is the man in charge, town mayor, party member, in boots, small but straight under his plumed hat, receives them, signs a paper, in short accepts delivery of him, tells him that he'll be put up in an attic room.

Three flights of steep stairs and the room is here, no fire but soon it will be spring, a chair and toilet, basin and pitcher.

The skylight looks out over the forest and the mountains in the distance, the hills, the border, from this point on Mathieu is ready to get down to the job out there, how is he going to pass through, by what path, custom's route, doesn't know the region at all, taking a big risk, doesn't realize the danger perhaps.

Is going to work things out, will surely pass through, half smile, didn't get himself caught this morning.

Hasn't reappeared, the traveler, didn't come back, the vagabond, to see if I was coming, retrace his steps, a bearer of what tidings, knew that I wouldn't be coming, that I wouldn't follow him, nor his idea, grand plan or absence of any ideas, likings, desires.

Passing through here was to give me a sign, what if he gave a sign to others this way and wasn't followed so far, knows it already, that nobody will follow him, which is what makes him laugh.

His age difficult to determine, is there an age for leaving, an age for staying and guarding the premises, keeping watch over the house, keeping watch all around the house?

An age for visiting, another for revisiting, reliving? How many places already revisited, places from the past, from childhood, adolescence, I reappeared without warning and strode around the area, rediscovered the gestures, the postures forged by the topography of the place, ghost gestures inside me, haunting my muscles, my nerves, my skin, phantoms from all other known places, incorporated small-scale and placed in suspension, tender reserve of worlds.

During that time, yes, that time of war, it really does seem that I lived over there, my body reads it, what is written inside it, it's beyond belief, no other connection with "here" but this reminiscence of the flesh, the mind's not much good for interlinking places, the story holds no force of proof.

No logic is much good but reflex has the force of law in this domain, the impetus salvaged, a precise automatism, the trace's red blood irrigating the veins, the imprints, the marks prone to reanimate what once was, once only, and replayed simply with a passing movement of the hand, of the neck by chance bowing, but then nothing is by chance.

He won't come back, learned a lot no doubt, much more than myself, knows how to erase the traces of his country, the traces of his footsteps, crossed the border, himself opened the outward-leading path.

Used no words, listened to mine and laughed, it wasn't mockery, for him, an ancient story, like this shadow passing over our part of the earth, already ancient for him, he foils the eclipse in his way, the only way.

I went back into the house, felt like having a drink, a smoke, went to look for some wine in the garage, a pack of tobacco, set myself up on the doorstep, drank, smoked, looked at that glimmer in the west, endlessly diminishing in gradations of yellow and red and deep purple, when all was little more than a shadowy glow beyond the mass of bushes I saw that the power had come back, the bulb was shining above the door.

I took my pipe and bottle and rushed into the living room, the very last night of electricity perhaps, put the cassette into the machine, I'd taken it out in anticipation, *Shoah*, the one I call "return," I reran it often.

A strange thing happened, in the first episode, between the body of the man and the field, in the opening of the field, too flat to his eyes, an essential thing, absent signs flow in, miss coinciding, the ground was turned over every autumn, flowers were gathered every spring, the pines at the edge have grown tall, Simon hesitates, looks for his way, doesn't understand, takes a few steps and evidently sight isn't much help to him, nor hearing, there weren't many birds at this location thirty years ago, touch has no object naturally, it's the measure of steps which sets him on course, a revived sensation, precise feeling of a distance traveled, a definite orientation, here a detour imposed by the obstacle long since removed, there an incline, a change in the nature of the soil underfoot.

Simon rediscovers his tracks, all the relationships between space and duration, the solicited specter replays the hand of cards, always wins hands down, the mute eye fixed motionless.

Tenacious lesson of this scene, which is not a scene, very simple, betting on duration, it was necessary to wait, not to force time, space becomes time in which space comes about by way of time roughly handled, ancient space in its buried duration, contorted by fragmentary traces no longer bearing the name of memory, the names of memory can speak now, sing, cantilena along the streaming water, from another age, age of childhood scoffed, no points of reference at that age, an assassinated age, ball and chain on the ankle, an age overwhelmed with horror.

The image suddenly vanishes, everything stops, is extinguished, the man over there—you never know—who's working the levers, or else the downed branches for one moment fallen still, no longer disturbing the line—has just sanctioned my sequence, I saw it one more time, the last time some will say, cassette in midviewing not rewound, is going to jam, will snap, tomorrow I'll try rewinding it by hand.

I go out of my living room, raising the drape, walk into the kitchen, light the candle, there must be a faint glimmer here somewhere at all times, carry it into the bedroom, transfer pipe and glass, move the chair closer to the open window and sit there, drinking, observing, listening.

Pitch-dark, the sky a great vibrant display, a quivering of leaves, in waves, with no ebb, the cuckoo, very far off, beyond the orchard no doubt, I relight my pipe, finish the bottle.

Hoo-hoo of the tawny owl, or else my ears are ringing, but no, it's the owl, very early this year, comes back only in September generally, perched in the plane tree.

The owl scans the summer night. If I'd left, I never would've known that it had come back; staying on sets up a batch of surprises.

Where is he spending his night, the devil's messenger, that poor man's Superman?

Rocky valley cutting a gash through the deep forest, ruined fortress in the northern mist, flowered village, horseman on the sinuous path going up to the castle, this is rustic Germanic country, Martin from the top of his skylight rediscovers it every morning, effortlessly identifies it.

Landscape steeped in childhood, he finally found it, more than a fairy-tale representation, a quotation, would be absorbed through its reading, its turns of phrase, this is the Germany of the past, the ideal land, out of books, the constraint that conducted him here, simulacrum or slip, he takes it for one of time's clever tricks.

He arrives at the station early, the one of the two employees who looks like he's the stationmaster makes him load the locomotives, it's backbreaking work to lift shovels full of coal so high, the makeshift railroad man arranges periods of rest for himself, takes things nice and easy, the others chat over there in the wooden shack.

Single track, two trains pass through here, morning and evening, after a week the one that came from the north no longer passes, the one from the south still comes up and doesn't go any farther, another week and no more trains at all, Martin puts in an appearance, then doesn't come back anymore, nobody says anything to him.

Takes his meals in the castle staff dining quarters, goes for walks in the forest, finds books in an attic and stays in his room reading, or goes down to the village, speaks with the farmers.

With the forester, listen to the news together, the Allied advance stopped at the Bavarian border, the man with the plume

regains confidence, new weapons, separate peace, hope nour-
ished by every German of an about-turn in alliances, Westerners
containing the "hordes" to the east, repulsing them.

Beginning of April, refugees from Prussia arrive in the village,
move in with the inhabitants, the majority in the castle, among
them Emmi and her mother, Emmi is a student, she goes for
walks in the woods, book in hand, meets Martin there.

Average height but slender, light chestnut hair, grey-blue eyes,
not shy, reserved, taciturn, passionate, then teasing and lively.

Martin is enamored of her as of one of those unpredictably
moody heroines, dissolving into tears at the slightest word,
elusive and proud. Emmi, at the very least, stamps the forest with
a seal of romanticism, discreet, classical, refined.

The valley vistas enchant her, she recites poetry, foiling the
echo, their escapes last forever, it takes a flight of bombers in
close formation to remind them of the war, the din can be heard
from here shortly afterward, upon some city on the plain, she
presses up against him, silent, reassured, her idea is that the
castle protects them.

The castle must be watched over, watched over, she repeats,
she lives in a tower, and once her mother is asleep, down the
narrow staircase she comes in the darkness and knocks at his
door. Open window in the night, they contemplate the pale glow
of the setting sun, the white streaks on the forest, the shimmering
display of the sky.

She speaks about the north, moors and marshes, dunes on the
enclosed sea, her childhood linked to the bare plain, never came
to this region, it's a foreign land for her, the people strike her as
suspicious, even hostile, the situation's to blame no doubt, this
exasperation, this time of hatred.

The offensive has resumed, the radio says so, and this recon-
naissance plane flying low over the village, all alone, veers on one
wing, comes back, taking photos perhaps, tricolor roundels in
plain sight, the forester follows them with amazement, nose in the
air, arms dangling, yes it's the end they seem to be saying, what

did you think, the hour has come, no miracles, turn tail, it's high time.

That evening, the first soldiers pass, about thirty, on foot, come up through the valley and stop at the castle, are hungry, thirsty, a captain scrutinizes the horizon through his binoculars, indifferent, almost relieved, no battle sounds, no machine guns, no cannons.

The captain and soldiers go off, pass down by the station, as if on a stroll, without hurrying, without turning around, the night is calm, Emmi, Martin keep their eyes peeled for glimmers in the distance, movements, signs, they see nothing, hear nothing, the silent army is drawing near, as in the theater, stealthily, in small dashes.

The plane comes back in the morning, lets out a volley of bullets on the valley, a little later young recruits pass through running, haggard, trembling, they're fourteen, fifteen years old, have thrown down their weapons, their SS uniforms make the forester squint, he himself conducts them along a footpath far from the village.

Noon, magnificent weather, splendid spring light, not a cloud in the sky, sharp, brilliant sunshine.

The Führer's portrait has disappeared from the vestibule, the flag from the office, insignia and pennants from the hallway, haven't been replaced yet, it's the moment of a rare vacancy and expectation, no more points of reference, the body in retreat, memories, each person holds back his voice, pricks up his ears.

Martin goes to post himself at the top of the tower to the west, stares wide-eyed, still can't make out anything, these instants trouble him, traps or tricks, they leave him uncertain, floating, he knows everything's going to topple, this country collapse, the unknown is right before him, still invisible, a new world, very different surely from what he knew in the past, he's going to return home, from exile, these words jostle inside him, switch places, combine.

Then he sees the flash in the sunlight where the path opens up, other flashes in the forest at the edge of the valley, the cannon stocks gleam, trained upon the village, the tanks are there, come to a halt.

They've been motionless for some time and Emmi stands straight up against the door at the summit of the tower, looks off into the distance, without seeing, comes very close to him, slips a book into his hands, remains pressed up against him a moment longer, draws back, goes off very quickly, the door slams, her steps echo on the stone stairs.

It's a collection of poems, *Last Greeting*, she wrote a few words on the endleaf: lots of luck for what's to come—everything that's coming, that's coming about now, that will become.

A racket out there covers the sound of her steps, smoke between the trees, the shell falls near the castle, two or three others more, then the cannons pivot, the tanks start moving, come down into the valley, they can be clearly heard at present, clank of tractor wheels, humming.

A lull, then the metallic commotion returns full force, the first vehicle appears where the forest ends, starts onto the road.

Martin came down from the tower, opened the portal below, went out onto the road and steps slowly forward, it's a great scene, he thinks, he saw it several times already, the guy walking alone in the broad sunlight, you don't know what's going to happen, suspense, close up, everyone's waiting.

The tank halted at the entrance to the village, covered with branches, five or six soldiers are perched on the vehicle, submachine gun in hand, helmets camouflaged with leaves, another following, revolver in his fist, takes an instrument out of his pocket and speaks.

He talks into a small box topped with an antenna, in a loud voice, stressing each syllable, another voice answers him, nasal, far off, seemingly from another world, Martin is staggered, Martians, he whispers, he never saw that before, that weapon, the others didn't have it!

He's very close now, the Martian calls out to him, soldiers, in the castle, are there still any, repeat, in the castle, soldiers, are there still any, repeat.

Martin understands in the end, musters up his three words of English, answers that there aren't any soldiers over there, there never were any, just a forester without a uniform.

Leaden sky, this morning, curiously smooth, even, cool weather, not raining however, woke up late, going for a stroll to get warm, on the road to the cave, overgrown now, a footpath has been cut over the former roadway.

Cut through the woods level with the *caselle*, climb to the hill-top, come back almost running, jumping over the low walls, I have the houses in sight once again, sit down on the rock at the edge of the field.

It's the squirrels' path, they come from the wood along here, along the tops of the walls, branches, cautiously pass over the intersection of the cross, always the same route, the same distance traveled.

Eat hazelnuts, all nuts, hide them in the loose soil, forget the spot, walnut tree nurseries everywhere in the direction of the orchard, drink the birds' water, familiar, observing me.

Gorge themselves on elm seeds, take enormous risks venturing to the tips of branches, journey back sometimes along the lawn, walking on all fours in the lane, legs spread, backsides up in the air.

Their courses guided by immutable landmarks, points of reference for gathering, transit, rest, the fixed distances animals travel, I inscribe my own trajectories through these networks, my tracks mingle with theirs, cut across them, often double and scramble them, the only human passing that way, the only competitor, rival, stamping his mark on earth and wood, sand, stone.

The only rival for a long time, partner as well, nobody knows where it will end, this depopulation, off in the distance, or internal intimate exile, I'm here for a little while longer, an eye out for problems.

Keeping all things in working condition as far as possible, in good condition, I set down to my task with diligence, knowledge, the little that I've learned is here, if someone comes later on I'll tell him this is what I've learned, this is what I know how to do.

Or nobody will come the whole time I'm here, those who'll pass through later on will find the house, if it isn't in ruins yet, sunk under the brambles, open it up and say, oh, somebody used to live here, he knew how to do this, that, people knew how to do such things, back then, how strange.

Noon, grey sky, looks like the daylight's failing, or my eyesight, take very good care of my glasses, soon I won't be able to do without them perhaps, refind the case while waiting, when I see clearly again.

And turn over the soil, dig, hoe at last, water, weed, you don't really need to be a magician, a vegetable patch in the orchard over there, carrots, radishes, lettuce, tomatoes, sweet potatoes, soon I'll run out of things to exchange at this rate, the others too for that matter, and perhaps before me.

Not to think about winter, work, labor here, one day at a time, modest horizon, keep attentive watch over the house, repair it, maintain it, inspect the walls, roofing, framework, fireplaces, sweep them out.

Keep the appliances in working order, clean them, check them, power back on without warning, you never know, not one station is broadcasting, no doubt, communications broken down, stillborn, short-circuited frequencies, sound and images, Walkman, walkie-talkie, cable and tube, satellites, emptied of every reflection, every resonance, each man reduced to his own organ, to being within earshot, last cry of the media.

I can shout myself hoarse, nobody will hear me, narrow target audience, zero percentage of listeners, only the animals, they'll crouch down, lift their noses, taken aback, after some time will grow used to it, won't pay any more attention, will continue along their ways as if nothing had happened.

Weasel in the high walls, civet in the roof, between ceiling and tiles, your large protruding eyes, pointy nose, round ears, with your long tail slink like a snake along the walls, drop down them vertically, your young play in the springtime, create a hellish row.

The hedgehog, the mole, the very long, very fat viper, at the edge of the *causse*.

This is the place to be, the best spot around here, large field of observation, the small house set slightly down below, the pond a little to the right, the large house standing high and clear, all paths of access visible, big road, cave, a farm with the dog.

This is where I must settle down, yes, on this rock, one glance takes in the surroundings, nobody else can see me, except if stumbling upon me by accident, tumbling down from the *causse*, using guesswork, groping along, on the blind.

In the darkness. A strange obscurity has come to drape all forms, all colors, it's not night, a veil of gloom has interposed itself, I still see everything through this screen, not murky, but a little faded, with diminished brightness, as if due to a loss of daylight, this has never happened, in living memory.

Imposing effect of false night, frightening, a contrived darkness, catches me short, a shadow is passing over the earth, what an accelerated phenomenon, system off kilter, everything was headed in this direction perhaps, all these past years.

Obscuration.

Wait, don't move from this spot, the shadow is growing, I'd get lost, lose my footing, stay here whatever comes about, eyes watchful, stand guard by the house.

With watchful eyes, peeled for what awakening in my wakeful watch?

Something else has begun perhaps.